To Shannon
Best Wishes
[signature]

Also by Jerome Arthur

Antoine Farot and Swede
Down the Foggy Ruins of Time
Life Could be a Dream, Sweetheart
One and Two Halves
The Journeyman and the Apprentice
The Death of Soc Smith
The Finale of Seem
Oh, Hard Tuesday
Got no Secrets to Conceal
Brushes with Fame

The Muttering Retreats

A Novel

Jerome Arthur

To my daughter Kimberley Peake,
who has been there, but with better luck.

The Muttering Retreats

Published by Jerome Arthur
P.O. Box 818
Santa Cruz, California 95061
831-425-8818
www.JeromeArthurNovelist.com
Jerome@JeromeArthurNovelist.com

Acknowledgments

Thanks to Don Rothman for editorial assistance, and D.K. Pierstorff for the poem "Holdorff's Reply." Cover design by Sherri Goodman.

One

Holdorff knew when he got to the Santa Cruz campus of the University of California that time was running out. In the seventeen years since he'd been discharged from the Navy, he'd been enrolled at four colleges. It had only taken him four years to get his B.A. degree. He graduated at the midterm from Long Beach State College and signed a contract for the spring semester teaching English at a Long Beach high school. Midway through that semester, he was accepted as a candidate in the M.A. program in American literature at the Southern Division of the University of Nevada in Las Vegas, his first venture into graduate school. He started the program in the fall.

The summer after his first year at S.D.U.N., he got a job dealing blackjack at the Pioneer Club on Fremont Street in downtown Las Vegas. One night at the start of his third semester, as he was dealing cards, a small-town school administrator sat down at his table and played till Holdorff's shift ended. Then after filling him up with beer, he signed him to a teaching contract in the small desert town of Needles, California.

The Needles job was short-lived. He started it the second week of the fall semester and stayed till the end of the school year. About two days after he arrived, he sobered up enough to realize his mistake, and made up his mind to get out of there at the end of his contract. He left Needles in June and headed back to Long Beach and the job he worked in his student days in the produce department of the A & P in Belmont Shore. In the fall he got a teaching assistantship in the M.A. program at State. By the end of that school year, he'd been accepted in the Ph.D. program at the University of Southern California. Holdorff never truly understood why he even applied for this program, and he most certainly did not know how he ever got accepted. After all, his original goal was to get a master's degree so that he could get a job teaching junior college English.

The next, and last, stop in his academic odyssey was Santa Cruz. Once again, he wasn't sure why he made this move. His main interest was the university. He hadn't lived more than a

The Muttering Retreats

mile or two from a college campus since he got out of the Navy, and he'd never had much trouble getting into any of them. But things were different at Santa Cruz. He couldn't get in.

"You can't hesitate," he'd said many times over the years. "Just walk in and act like you belong, act like you're a member of the club, and nobody'll question you. Hesitate just once, and they'll peg you for a fraud, and you're done."

Whenever he thought he was on the road to achieving his objectives, something would get in the way. At Southern Nevada, he alienated his committee when he hooked his wagon to Roget's star. Roget was his faculty adviser there. The return to Long Beach was only a stopgap, although it shouldn't have been. If he'd stuck it out and gotten his M.A. degree, he might have had a good chance of getting a job at City, Compton College, or any number of other junior colleges in the Los Angeles basin and Orange County. The U.S.C. experience took the biggest toll on his psyche. He put in the most years there and still came away empty handed. No one was more surprised than he was that he even got in the school. He really didn't expect to get accepted there, and even he realized after a couple semesters that he probably shouldn't have been.

The treatment he got at Santa Cruz didn't come as a surprise to him. He couldn't even register as an undergraduate, much less be accepted in the graduate program or get a teaching assistantship. The best he could do was unofficially audit classes in subjects he'd already taken, some of them more than once. But he kept at it, attempting at the start of each new quarter (so far he'd been trying for over two years) to get enrolled.

He liked the innovative atmosphere at the school, but this only added to his problem. Because of its innovations, it was a popular college, so enrollments flourished. Thus, it was virtually impossible for a well-traveled scholar like Holdorff to receive preferred treatment over promising young graduates from some of the most prestigious universities in the country. He still clung to the distant hope that he might some day be accepted as a graduate student or even better yet as a lecturer because of all the different teaching assistantships. Also, he thought the publication of two of his poems in a little magazine called *Moondog* should count for something. Not to mention the thousands of other poems he'd written as well as the lyrics to hun-

The Muttering Retreats

dreds of popular songs that he'd tried to peddle unsuccessfully to various agents in Hollywood whose addresses he'd found in *Literary Marketplace*.

His writing was perhaps the biggest impediment to his getting an advanced degree. If he got the urge to sit down and write, he would relinquish all other obligations and immerse himself in whatever idea he was developing at the time. He once tried to write a paper entitled "the linguistic significance of lower case letters in the poetry of e.e. cummings," and as usual, he got sidetracked and wound up writing a satirical poem about the subject. He thought of himself as a genuine poet and lyricist. No slick hype or phony intellectual scam for him. Just honest-to-god poetry and song lyrics. He wrote for the love of writing, storing the originals of reams of unpublished, but finished and highly polished verse in his refrigerator.

"If my house ever burns down," he'd say, "all my poems and songs'll be saved. I may die in the blaze, but my writing will live on after I'm gone."

That's how he talked when he was young, but the older he got, the more cynical he became, and in later years he had the feeling that his words would never be read or sung by

11

anybody. He made carbon copies of everything, and he would put those in a wooden outbox that he kept next the ancient Underwood typewriter that sat on the kitchen table of whatever apartment he was living in. He usually waited till he had at least a hundred poems (enough for a book) in the stack before he submitted them. He did the songs a little differently. In the late 'fifties when the long playing album became the standard in the recording industry, Holdorff noticed that most albums had about ten cuts total, five on each side. So he'd send off ten songs at a time to different Hollywood and New York agents. Most of them came back to him, sometimes opened, but most of the time not. Whenever they did come back, he'd put them in a new nine-by-twelve manila envelope and send them to another name on his list. Some of the carbons of the verse he wrote went to the few people to whom he dedicated them.

Over the years he had a recurring dream, nightmare would be a more appropriate word for it, in which he died in a blaze in his apartment, and from somewhere overlooking it, he saw fire investigators sifting through the debris until they stumbled upon the refrigerator, emptied its contents and swept them away

The Muttering Retreats

When he failed his comprehensive exams at U.S.C., he wrote a poem to the graduate dean expressing his outrage at the treatment he was getting. There were five professors on his graduate committee, and only one of them knew anything about T.S. Eliot, which was Holdorff's specialty. The other committee members were linguistics and romantics and Renaissance scholars.

He'd been asked to explicate the first seventeen lines from the second section of T.S. Eliot's "The Waste Land" ("right up my alley"). He considered himself to be an Eliot expert. The point of his explication was that the passage is a parody of the scene from Shakespeare's *Antony and Cleopatra* in which Enobarbus describes Cleopatra sailing her sumptuous and lavish barge. He thought he'd argued persuasively in his paper that Eliot's language clearly showed that he was poking fun at Shakespeare's elevated verse style. After all, Holdorff pointed out, wasn't Eliot really describing a twentieth century call girl with "her strange synthetic perfumes,/Unguent, powdered, or liquid troubled, confused/And drowned the sense in odours"? What else could Eliot be doing but satirizing the elegant, tragic, elevated, dramatic picture that Shakespeare had painted? Holdorff took the satire angle one step further and wrote that Cleopatra herself was merely a high class whore, a woman "O'erpicturing that Venus where we see/The fancy out-work nature."

That explication was Holdorff's undoing at U.S.C. He was failed outright by the committee and told that he would not be permitted to petition to take the comprehensives again. But that didn't stop him. He got possession of the exam, and with his adviser's blessing, he went to each member of the committee and questioned him/her on specific points of his essay. There were three men and two women on the committee. One of the women had taken off to Europe on sabbatical leave, so, mercifully, Holdorff didn't talk to her, but he made the rounds of all the others.

The first one he spoke to was a Wordsworth/Coleridge scholar, who, when Holdorff questioned him, admitted not having read "The Waste Land." The second committee member he spoke to, Amsterdam, taught courses in freshman composition only. He hadn't taught a literature course in five years. The only reason he was even on the committee was because he was the coordinator of the graduate program in literature. He pleaded innocence to failing Holdorff. In fact, he suggested to the committee that

The Muttering Retreats

that they pass him because he knew Holdorff would protest the failing grade. Amsterdam told Holdorff that he didn't stand a chance of getting the committee's unanimous decision reversed.

The third committee member he approached was a linguist, and her only comment to him was, "I'm a linguist, and I don't even understand literary interpretation. I merely went along with the other members of the committee." There was such finality, such intransigence in her tone that Holdorff felt like his balls had been cut off. He began to think he was lucky that the other woman on the committee, a short, overweight English Renaissance scholar with bulbous varicose veins popping out at her knee joints, had gone to Europe, thus relieving him of having to deal with her.

The only member who could have known what Holdorff was doing, and therefore could have defended his thesis before the committee, had his own reasons for failing him. He was an American lit. scholar whose doctoral dissertation had been on the Latinate words in Wallace Stevens' poetry. He failed him because he believed Stevens was a better poet than Eliot and he resented Eliot's popularity in academic circles. He rejected anything that was done by anybody about T.S. Eliot. Once again Holdorff had been in the wrong place at the wrong time.

Thus outraged and injured, he wrote a poem. He always wrote a poem or a song when he got desperate, when there was no further recourse, when all avenues were exhausted. Poetry was his vent. After all, if Ab Snopes could burn a man's barn down over a lousy hundred-dollar rug, why couldn't Holdorff write a poem to express his own indignation? So, he grabbed a couple of the cancelled postal envelopes he carried around in the breast pocket of his corduroy sports jacket and dashed off "Holdorff's Reply." Then he slipped a clean sheet of white paper and a carbon copy into his Underwood and transcribed the poem:

> Dear Dr. Amsterdam (and other ships at sea)
> I hope you haven't figured
> That you got the best of me
> By keeping me from ending
> Academic poverty.
> (You knew I wanted to pass my test
> And that I gave it my level best,
> So you played the game called "cats and mouse."
> Still I don't feel that you're a louse.)
> No, my kind sir, contrary
> To that, I feel you've made me free:
> This mouse has left; now all you'll see
> Are frightened mice, led by Mickey.

The Muttering Retreats

And when they cry and try to plea
I know that you will think of me
And pass them all with accolades
Giving degrees despite the grades.
And so I'll know (henceforth it's true)
That I've passed more Ph.D.s than you.

He felt so inspired by this burst that he wrote an afterword:

There is no greater Humanity
In all of U.S.C.
Than that existing just for me
In the department of humanities.

For that's where Amsterdam resides
Who neither compliments nor
    derides
Anything I give to him:
He considers me a minor whim.

Two

Holdorff thought his life boiled down to two things: writing verse, and going to school. Both activities were second nature to him, like eating and sleeping. He'd been doing them so long that if he quit either or both, he wouldn't know what else to do with himself. Nothing he'd ever done in life, except perhaps giving birth to his son, Humphrey, had given him as much satisfaction as learning new things and formulating them into the organic unit of a poem or song. Certainly not working the produce counter at the A & P in his undergraduate years or teaching high school English, although there was a certain amount of fulfillment in the classroom experience.

"It's all true. Pushing produce doesn't cut it, but pushing chalk has its good points," he'd said when he came home to Long Beach from the desert and went back to work at the A & P. "The only bad part of teaching is when you got'a deal with the administration. Nothing beats putting words on the page to tell a story or elicit an emotional response. Nothing."

The only other thing that was more rewarding was having a son and watching him grow. He was the only family Holdorff ever claimed, the one positive thing to come from his brief marriage.

As a child, he himself was left to his own devices after his mother died and his father took to drink. It was all he could do to wait till he graduated from high school so he could strike out on his own. He was eighteen, old enough to go all by himself to the Navy recruiter in the post office across Alameda Street from Olvera Street, and join up. The last time he saw his father was when he said one last goodbye to him at Union Station as he boarded the train on his way to boot camp in San Diego.

After he completed two months of basic training, he went to corpsman school. He managed to get stationed stateside for the next two years, and in the spring of 'fifty-two, he shipped out to a M*A*S*H unit in Korea where he stayed until he got wounded in the fall. He'd been sent to the front as the war was winding down. Wearing a Red Cross helmet and carrying a first aid kit, he crawled on his stomach and dragged wounded soldiers back behind the lines where he tried to patch them up and return them to battle or send them home depending on how serious the wound. Holdorff picked up some shrapnel in the back from a stray American grenade and was back in the States before Thanksgiving.

"What they call friendly fire," he later scoffed. "Sounds like an oxymoron to me."

An Army doctor implanted plastic in his back at Letterman Hospital at the Presidio in San Francisco. He mustered out with an eighty percent disability.

In the Navy Holdorff learned that the most incompetent people were always the ones passing out the orders. The more capable you were, the more subordinate you became. In Holdorff's view the worst part of that arrangement, in a military context, was that incompetence determined whether capability and skill lived or died. Another thing he learned from his military service was that the people who made the most money and had the easiest jobs were college graduates. That's when he first thought it might be a good idea to get a college education. His G.I. benefits plus his disability pension made it financially practical for him to do it.

The Muttering Retreats

The seed for writing poetry was planted as he was convalescing at Letterman, but it was so incipient at that stage that he hardly noticed it. It really began to blossom when he read "The Love Song of J. Alfred Prufrock" in English 1B at Long Beach City College. That wasn't the first time he'd read the poem, but it was the first time he read it under Tavisón's supervision. He was the first college teacher to spark Holdorff's interest in English and literature.

Tavisón was a high school dropout who'd enlisted in the Marine Corps at the end of the Second World War. He impressed Holdorff with his simple, down-to-earth manner. Tavisón had only recently become interested in poetry himself, studying it in graduate school because he wanted to understand it better. Holdorff liked his easy, unpretentious approach to literature. That simplicity, especially as applied to "Prufrock," was Holdorff's first major inspiration. To Holdorff the poem spoke for itself, but after Tavisón lectured on it, Holdorff thought it had to be one of the best poems written in the twentieth century.

So, he seriously set out to write his own poems, imitating and later emulating Eliot and others: Pound, Stevens and Frost to name only a few. Then he started reading his contemporaries, the Beats: Ginsberg, Ferlinghetti and Corso, and from these he developed his sardonic bent, an inclination that began during his stay at Letterman. He could sit down and read "Howl" or "Loud Prayer," and before he knew what he was doing, he'd be dashing off a lyric poem that, he thought, expressed all his own rage and fury and anger.

Sometimes Holdorff couldn't write if his life depended on it. He'd take his brown plastic, tiger-striped glasses off, and sit staring at the wall for long periods of time, trying to think of something to put down. When this happened, he'd pick up a collection of poems by Wordsworth or Coleridge or Eliot or Stevens, *anybody*, he didn't care, and he'd read their stuff for inspiration, and if none came, then he'd just start writing random rhymes:

Got'a be Someplace

I fill up a blank sheet
With words that repeat
All that's ever been said
And most of what's been read.

Or I end up not even caring,
Rather just sit blankly staring
Over at the plain bare wall

The Muttering Retreats

Waiting for the words to fall.

One night shortly after his twentieth high school reunion, he sat for two hours trying to think of something appropriate to write about the occasion. The reunion had been a great success, a touching affair. All the guys he'd known back then were settled down and prospering, and that had made him feel good on their account. They were making him feel good about himself, even though *he* didn't really think there was much to feel good about. By that time he was at the end of his academic rope. It was all over.

"Sure is good to see you again," said Garfield at the reunion. "Had to come when I heard *you* were go'n'a be here."

"Yeah, me too," echoed Rodney and Graff.

"Thanks," Holdorff said. "Good to see you guys, too."

Then after they told him what they were doing with their lives, he told them about his adventures in academia and about his writing. They praised him for having more education than all of them put together, and they envied him his song writing and poetry. They also said he was looking better than he looked twenty years ago, which was true.

In high school he was just a skinny kid. Holdorff had filled out over the years, but he wasn't by any means overweight, despite his heavy beer consumption, (he figured it was his hyperactive personality that kept him so slim), and at first sight he looked a little more distinguished than rumpled with his graying reddish hair and beard. It was only after you spoke to him and saw him up close in his tan corduroy sport jacket with leather patches on the elbows that you realized he was a disheveled, eccentric intellectual. He gesticulated with his pipe stem as he cupped the bowl in the palm of his right hand, the whole time holding a match over it with the thumb and forefinger of the same hand until he almost singed himself. Between gestures he took drags, blowing each one out his nose while at the same time inhaling succeeding puffs.

Holdorff was sure that his former classmates were sincere, but he also thought there was a good chance they were complimenting him out of politeness. And then maybe they weren't, because some of them also looked much better at the reunion than they did twenty years earlier. Especially some of the women.

The Muttering Retreats

The ones he'd remembered being beauties as teenagers had become overweight and neurotic, while the ones he and his buddies thought were unattractive in high school had grown into classy, cosmopolitan women with brains, bright smiles and smooth, natural looking clothes on their slim bodies. The lucky guys they were married to!

"Any of you guys hear anything about Weaver? How come he's not here?" Holdorff asked. Weaver was his best friend in high school.

"I actually called him and personally invited him," said Garfield, "but he said he just didn't wan'a come. Said it was something out of his past and what's past is done. Don't look back."

This was a big disappointment to Holdorff. If he ever thought of anybody as a brother, it was Weaver. His first idea as he sat there trying to think of a poem was to write a lament for not having seen him, but he knew that wouldn't do because it wouldn't express the total feeling of the reunion.

His next thought was to do a series of songs to the other friends he'd talked to at the reunion, like, for example, a lyric poem to Flowers, who, he was sure, was a homosexual.

25

Oh indeed, he had come to the reunion with his wife of twenty years who had been his high school sweetheart, but he'd made a few comments and done a couple things that, Holdorff thought, proved he was queer as a tree full of fish. At one point during the cocktail hour, he asked Holdorff if he could hug him, to which Holdorff replied, "Sure." Then he squeezed Holdorff so sensuously that it left little doubt in his mind what Flowers' sexual orientation was.

"I got'a be careful," Flowers said. "My wife gets jealous when she sees me talking too much to guys."

The topper was when Flowers left the party, he kissed Holdorff right on the mouth, which, being kissed by another man, was a first for Holdorff. He saw a certain irony in Flowers' homosexuality. In their junior year, the two of them had gone to a Turkish bathhouse one night on a lark, and they had met an older gentleman there who was obviously a homosexual. Holdorff remembered very clearly how Flowers had condemned the man for being perverted and now here he was, approaching middle age, making passes at men and worrying about his wife's jealousy.

A series of poems wasn't what he wanted because it wouldn't seize upon the total experience of the reunion. He needed something that would capture it, but he couldn't find it. All he could do was think of specific individuals and how his reunion with them had gone. There was the guy who'd been a really cool cat, quiet and unassuming, not really popular, but one of the ones no one disliked. He'd approached Holdorff after the dinner and called him by his first name.

"Sure is good to see yuh," he said. "You seen Ochs lately?"

"God, I haven't seen him since we graduated," Holdorff replied. After Weaver, Ochs was Holdorff's second best buddy. "You seen him lately?"

"Yeah, one morning a couple months ago. Down at the Pantry. Went there for breakfast, and there he was. I've actually seen him from time to time over the years. Doin' real good. Got a job as a social worker."

"Good deal. How come he's not here?"

"I tried to talk him into it, but he just said he didn't wan'a spend the dough."

"Too bad. Would'a' been good to see 'im."

Holdorff went completely blank on the guy's name. He took a stab at it and came up wrong, but the guy only winced slightly and acted normal, pretended Holdorff had called him by his right name. Then he just kind of faded off, and Holdorff didn't see him again for the rest of the night. That was the first face he looked up in his yearbook when he got home, and he found that he wasn't even close to the right name.

"What the hell," he said. "I'll probably never see the guy again, anyway."

He was bewildered by his loss of memory of late, sloughing it off in this manner, unwilling to face the larger reality of it.

There he sat for two hours, pen in hand over a cancelled envelope. Suddenly, his eyes focused on the bookshelf straight ahead five feet from where he sat. He saw the copy of the *Bob Dylan Song Book*, so he got up, walked over and got it out. He flipped the pages to the index and found a song he'd remembered from a few years before. "Bob Dylan's Dream." Page sixty-six.

"This is it!" he said, as he read.

It was so good that tears began to well up in his eyes. He wished he'd had it there to read to the entire reunion. Clearly, it was something they would have understood. It was so much like how it really had been. So what if his best friend (his brother?) didn't show up? Or that another good friend had gone gay and started hustling him? Or that he couldn't remember another friend's name? They could read these song lyrics and really understand what was happening.

He walked over to the apple crate where he kept his collection of L.P.s. He found *The Freewheelin' Bob Dylan*, walked it over to his portable Webcor record player and set the flip side face up on the spindle. He dropped the arm down onto the record, and the needle came to rest on the first track, "Bob Dylan's Dream." He read the lyrics again as the song played, and once again, tears came to his eyes. When the song ended, he sat down at the table, and with Shakespeare's "Sonnet Eighteen" in mind, he began to write, dashing off an Elizabethan sonnet of his own, which was unusual for him; he didn't like to confine himself to such a rigid structure. But this time the pieces all fell into place, and when he completed the poem on the envelope, he moved to the chair in front of his Underwood and transcribed it in original, plus carbon copy:

Ode on a Reunion

Had a dream I saw you guys, my ol' pals.
It was only a buncha' guys who showed;
Not anybody else who came were gals.

Jerome Arthur

It felt like I had hit the mother lode
Of my fondest dear old reminiscence.
In the dream I was completely speechless.
Don't know why; I had lots of confidence.
I was sixteen again, I must confess.
If we could only go back in real life
To when we were so young and innocent,
And we could ditch all this modern day strife,
Indeed I'd give up even my last cent.
  But I know that such a thing can't be real
  No matter how I try to make the deal.

When he was done, he got up from the typewriter and paced around reading the finished work. Then he walked over to the refrigerator and deposited the original on top of the stack. He was thinking there must be close to five thousand sheets of paper there. A sense of accomplishment flooded him as he thought about it. He closed the refrigerator door, walked the carbon over to the outbox, deposited it, sat down at the table, lit his pipe and took five big puffs. Then he killed off the last swallow of beer and went to bed.

Three

Holdorff met an Aviation Machinist's Mate while he was recuperating from his back wound at Letterman. His name was Rheinhardt, and whenever Holdorff saw him, he had an armload of books, usually not the ones from the base library, but rather books he brought in from the outside. These were books that wouldn't be found in the base library. Among them were Bertrand Russell's *Why I am not a Christian*, Plato's *Apology* and Geoffrey Chaucer's *The Canterbury Tales*. Rheinhardt was the best-read person Holdorff had ever met. He was one of those geniuses who was not understood or appreciated by most of his peers. Holdorff thought of himself that way. He felt that he had a lot in common with Rheinhardt.

One time Holdorff was wheeling his chair down a corridor when suddenly he overheard someone talking up ahead around the corner. As he wheeled silently toward the sound, he

Jerome Arthur

perceived it to be two voices carrying on a conversation. As he came upon the bend in the hall, he saw that it was Rheinhardt standing over another patient, prone on a gurney, sedated and unconscious. Before Rheinhardt got a look at him, Holdorff backed his wheelchair up and peeked around the corner. Tucked under Rheinhardt's arm were his ubiquitous books. Holdorff watched and listened as Rheinhardt carried on both sides of the conversation, asking the unconscious guy questions and then projecting his voice like a ventriloquist to make it sound like the guy was answering him.

Holdorff watched as Rheinhardt kept the conversation going. After about three minutes, a Corpsman appeared, shook his head at Rheinhardt as though he thought he was some kind of a nut, and rolled the unconscious patient on the gurney away.

"Wow!" Holdorff said as Rheinhardt passed him. "You're as good as Edgar Bergen. You could be in movies."

Rheinhardt simply went on his way holding up his right index finger and quoting:

> Neither cast ye your pearls before swine,
> Lest they trample them under their feet,
> And turn again and rend you.

The Muttering Retreats

The two books tucked under his arm were a paperback and a heavy, hardbound anthology entitled *Writers of the Western World.* Rheinhardt went back to his ward, sat on his bunk and kept his own counsel, quietly perusing his books.

He'd been injured trying to earn extra pay on a mission he didn't have to fly. Posted at the Naval Air Station, Alameda, on an island in the San Francisco Bay, he was a crewmember on a P2V that crash-landed back at the base after a routine patrol along the San Mateo coast in the country's ongoing anti-submarine warfare program that began during the Second World War. All nine crewmembers survived the crash, but Rheinhardt was the only one who sustained injuries and was shipped to Letterman.

He was certainly the most interesting person Holdorff met on his tour of duty. He was the most intelligent and the best educated, albeit self-educated, man he knew. It was his first taste of scholarly pursuits, and it whetted his appetite for more. His association with Rheinhardt was perhaps the biggest influence on his decision to go to college, even though Rheinhardt himself had not gone, and wasn't necessarily recommending that Holdorff go. Holdorff wanted

33

more. He didn't think he could do it the way Rheinhardt did it. He didn't have the self-discipline. He felt he needed the guidance of teach-errs and a curriculum and deadlines for tests and term papers.

The other thing that motivated Holdorff to go to college was the realization that the people who got the best treatment in the Navy were the officers, and they were usually college educated. That didn't necessarily mean they were any smarter than the non-college-graduate officers or the enlisted men. On the contrary, most of the time, the enlisted people were a lot smarter than the officers. Rheinhardt was a good example of that. Nor did it mean that they got any more respect, except maybe a false respect, but they got better treatment, just as he would learn later that the professors got better treatment than their students. So he could clearly see after sometime into his hitch that he needed a college education, and by the end of the two months with Rheinhardt in the military hospital, he was ready to get one.

Rheinhardt was Holdorff's kind of people, and Holdorff knew he wanted to be like him. So during the two months that he recuperated in San Francisco, he followed Rheinhardt around like a puppy, learning, in a general way,

The Muttering Retreats

about the golden age of Greece, the middle ages, the Renaissance, and modern philosophy, history and literature. Rheinhardt introduced Holdorff to a whole new world he knew nothing about.

One afternoon they were outside together on the grounds of the hospital, lounging around, enjoying the rare sunny day in San Francisco. Holdorff was in his wheelchair, and Rheinhardt was spread out on the lawn with his books in front of him. He was fifteen years older than Holdorff. He had a dark complexion, curly graying dark hair and a dark mustache with flecks of gray in it. He was a lifer (career man) with only four years until he could retire. It had puzzled Holdorff that such an intelligent man should choose the Navy for a career. He thought a guy like that would really be stifled in the narrow-minded confines of the military mentality. He thought almost anything, even a job with the phone company, would be better than the military, especially for someone with as active a mind as Rheinhardt's.

"Why'd yuh decide on a career in the Navy?" Holdorff asked as he lit his pipe.

He'd made it all through high school and two years in the service without picking up a smoking habit, and it was only the boredom and inactivity of the hospital that made him take up the pipe.

"I didn't really decide. Reason I joined in the first place, it was 'thirty-seven, middle of the Depression. Military was the only work I could find. I was all ready to get out when the japs bombed Pearl Harbor. Got extended for the duration. Time the war ended, I had eight years under my belt, so I figured what the hell? Almost half way to retirement. I'm a lazy son-of-a-bitch to boot. Let's face it, you're lazy, you can loaf for twenty years and get a pension when it's over. So that's what I been doin' till this plane crash. Always had easy duty, and got to travel all over the world. Did a Med. cruise and got to check out all those places I read about in Homer. My favorite character in *The Iliad* and *The Odyssey* is Odysseus, and I got to sail around all those places he traveled to get home, and Uncle Sam paid for the trip."

"But how can yuh take orders from these jerks who ain't half as smart as you? Don't yuh just wan'a tell 'em to shove it when they order yuh to do somethin' yuh know is stupid?"

"I've studied a little eastern religion and philosophy, and I know how to turn it off. I know the only reality is right here," Rheinhardt replied, pointing at his temple. "I've managed to

The Muttering Retreats

hold on for sixteen years, four of which were during the war, and I only have four to go. I'm go'n'a find myself a place here in San Francisco after I retire. There's a whole new thing happenin' here right now. Buncha' poets call themselves Beats. Hang out in North Beach. Hip bookstore called City Lights. I'll take you there sometime if we ever get liberty outa' this joint."

Rheinhardt had never married and didn't have any children, any that he knew of, that is. He'd bedded prostitutes from Wespac. to the Mediterranean, and party-time women in ports on both coasts of the United States. He'd had a couple long-term relationships that he eventually broke off because the women kept pressuring him to get married. He wasn't sure what kind of permanent relationship he wanted, if any, but he did know that he didn't want to get married. Most of the married couples he'd known over the years were bored, and he didn't want any part of that. He substituted his books for female companionship.

"He's married to his books," people who thought they knew him would say, and that was perhaps the best description of him.

In Holdorff's mind, Rheinhardt's uniqueness defied description. The ventriloquist incident was a good example. It was completely unexpected, and to Holdorff, off the wall, but it was real, and it showed yet one more dimension of Rheinhardt. Holdorff began to imagine himself when he got to Rheinhardt's age, in his shoes, pacing around, making philosophical and intellectual pronouncements, and having some young, aspiring intellectual hanging on his every word. That part of the dream never would come true for Holdorff, but his meeting Reinhardt was the first step in that direction.

They hung around together for two months, and during that time, Rheinhardt gave Holdorff his standard lecture on the curse of the house of Atreus, how it started with Atreus serving the cooked limbs of Thyestes' children to Thyestes at a banquet; to Agamemnon's sacrificing his daughter Iphigenia at Aulus; to his murder by his wife Clytemnestra and her lover Aegisthus; to their murder by Agamemnon's and Clytemnestra's daughter Electra; and finally to the removal of the curse from Electra's younger brother, Orestes.

He'd often heard of the Oedipus complex, but never knew what it was until Rheinhardt told him the story. By the end of the two months, he still hadn't read a book, but when he was around Rheinhardt, he was like a sponge soaking up everything he said, every book title he mentioned. He'd even put some of what was going through his head on paper. He wrote short lyric poems, mostly about unrequited love. It was a beginning, although a sentimental one that hardly showed any of the acerbity of which he would eventually be so proud. At that stage he wrote stuff like:

If You Only Knew

If you only knew
What it is you do
To me, you'd take care
Not to share
Your many stories
Of transitory
Lovers. I knew you
Didn't ever mean to
Hurt my feelings
And send me reeling
With the pain of your
Leaving me to pour
Over my grief and
Be in this wasteland.

Holdorff and Rheinhardt were quite a pair at Letterman. None of the other patients or the hospital staff knew quite what to make of them. This was because none of those people had any knowledge or understanding of the things Holdorff was learning from Rheinhardt. Holdorff hadn't read "The Love Song of J. Alfred Prufrock" yet, and he didn't have the cynical bent that would later characterize his best poetry, but he was trying his hand at it anyway. He had plenty of time on his hands to do it and since, unlike the other patients, he didn't have anybody back home to write to, he wrote verse.

It was also at this time that he started to take an interest in the popular music of the day, rhythm and blues. There was a new label that had started recording just four years ago, Atlantic Records. All of the artists were black people who seemed to be making music for a young, white audience. That at least was the audience that was buying the records, so Holdorff, seeing the possibility of future popularity for himself, tried his hand at lyric writing.

Still Seems like Déjà Vu

When you left, I couldn't believe
That you were really sayin' goodbye,
So it took me sometime to grieve
Till I finally realized that it was I
Who should have said farewell first,
But I just couldn't bring myself to it.
Our relationship must've been cursed,
And I should've known not to do it.

The Muttering Retreats

(Refrain)
So how can I get on without tryin'
New things and still come away not cryin'.
Even when it's oh so new,
It still seems like déjà vu.

I didn't realize how little you knew me;
I took so much for granted.
I only saw what I wanted to see,
And didn't know you didn't know what I
wanted.
Now that it's over, and I'm all alone and blue,
You've gotten what you wanted the most,
And I must live with only a memory of you.
Without a doubt, you've lived up to your boast.
(Refrain)

Toward the end of their stay in the hospital, Holdorff and Rheinhardt got weekend liberty. Holdorff was no longer confined to a wheelchair and was now walking with a cane. He was still moving a bit slowly, but he could get around fairly well. Rheinhardt's injury was a pulled muscle in his back. He was experiencing really bad lower back pain due to muscle spasms, and was mostly resting and recuperating. He'd been ambulatory throughout his stay in the hospital. Their liberty commenced at four-thirty on Friday afternoon, and they hopped on a San Francisco Muni streetcar at a quarter to five. They headed into town to Union Square. There, they got on the Powell Street cable car to Broadway and Columbus in North Beach.

They went straight to City Lights Books where they hung out and listened to a couple of poetry readings. The place was jumping with activity. Holdorff stuck close to Rheinhardt as they moved up and down the aisles looking at books. Rheinhardt was like a kid in a candy store, but he knew what he was looking for so he went straight to it. Holdorff was awestruck and simply looked at the selection in wonder. They spent most of the next couple hours pulling books off the shelves and looking at them. On Rheinhardt's recommendation Holdorff picked up copies of "The Love Song of J. Alfred Prufrock" and "The Wasteland" in one paper back volume, as well as a Penguin Classic of Twain's *The Adventures of Huckleberry Finn.* Rheinhardt got a copy of Byron's *Don Juan.*

"Been wanting to get a copy of this for a long time," he said as they stood in line at the cashier.

They hit a couple bars after they left the bookstore. Since they'd been getting their checks regularly in the hospital, with no place to spend the money, they were both flush when they got that liberty. The bathhouse they wound up in was quite nice. After soaking in a hot tub, they were escorted by two beautiful women into rooms in the back where they got massages and their sexual fantasies indulged. What a great night it had been!

On Monday morning orders came in for Holdorff to be transferred to the hospital ship *Haven* at Terminal Island in Long Beach where he would be released from active duty. Rheinhardt was reassigned to his old squadron at Alameda Naval Air Station. As they were packing their gear and getting ready to say their final goodbyes, Rheinhardt told Holdorff that he should get enrolled at Long Beach City College. It wasn't far from where he'd be getting his discharge.

"I was stationed down at Los Alamitos back in 'forty-eight and 'forty-nine, and I took a couple night classes at City. Had a world lit. class from a guy named Powers, and he really knows his stuff. It's a good school and a good place for you to start."

"All right," said Holdorff. "I really didn't have any idea what I was go'n'a do when I got out, so I guess I migh's well go there as anywhere. It's not far from where I grew up."

And so, Holdorff took a remedial English class at Long Beach City at night as he waited on board the *Haven* for his discharge. Although he was glad to be getting out of the Navy, he was already missing Rheinhardt, and though they swore they'd keep in touch, Holdorff never saw or heard from him after that last day at Letterman. As he waited to be processed out, he got the chance to look for an apartment, which he found in Belmont Shore. He bought a 'forty-seven Chevy Sedan Delivery for two hundred dollars, and was now poised and ready to begin his journey through the halls of academe. He put the Navy behind him, but he thought of Rheinhardt often.

Four

Holdorff mustered out of the Navy, and with an eighty percent disability and the G.I. bill, he registered as a full-time student at Long Beach City College. He'd soon found that the remedial English class he'd taken as he waited for his discharge was too easy, but he was glad he took it because it was where he met Tavisón, who picked up where Rheinhardt left off. Holdorff was the best student in the class, and Tavisón took him under his wing. He approached him as the semester was winding down.

"So, what're your plans?" Tavisón asked.

"Well, yuh know, I'm just getting outa' the Navy, and I'm go'n'a enroll here full-time spring semester."

"Okay, good. When you do, get into my English 11A class. I'm going to be needing you in there. It's a five unit class, and you'll be fulfilling your 1A and your speech requirements at the same time."

"Sounds good to me. What else should I take?"

"You'll need some general ed. courses like history and biology, foreign language, too, so be sure to get those into your program. Also, you're go'n'a need a counselor's signature. Just bring your schedule to me, and I'll sign it. I'll be your counselor." This was only Tavisón's second year at City, and he hadn't had much experience with counseling, but his credential indicated that he was qualified, and he had the confidence to do it. "Okay, so now you've told me what your short-term goals are. What're your plans for the long term?"

"Thought I'd be an English major. I wan'a do what you're doing, teach junior college English."

"Good, but I'd suggest one change, history instead of English."

"Why?"

"'Cause history's a lot easier than English. Only two objective tests a semester, a midterm and a final. You may have to assign the occasional research paper, but you won't be reading all those themes every week."

The Muttering Retreats

"Yeah, well, thanks for the advice, but I think I'll stick with English. More interesting than history."

Thus, Tavisón became Holdorff's second mentor, and Holdorff ended up taking at least one class from Tavisón during each of his four semesters at City. That spring he took the 11A class and got a B. He also took four units of beginning French for an A, three units of U.S. history for a C, and with those grades he made the dean's list.

Tavisón was a native Mexican who moved to Long Beach when he was a sophomore in high school. He was placed in a college prep track at Long Beach Poly, and one of his hardest classes was speech. As he nervously waited his turn at the back of the room, listening to the other students giving speeches, he'd dwell on his own flawed English, apprehensive about giving a speech because of it, but he was also determined to overcome that obstacle, so he did meticulous research—for a high school sophomore—on his subject: Hernán Cortés, Bernal Díaz del Castillo and the Aztecs. It was a subject he knew well, standard history fare in the school he'd gone to in Guadalajara. He polished up his final note cards and was ready to give what he thought was a good speech.

47

Jerome Arthur

When he got up in front of the class and started to speak, his deficiency in English was obvious, and some of his fellow students began to snicker. A couple minutes later, half the class was laughing. When he couldn't take anymore, he calmly gathered up his note cards from the lectern and walked out. That evening when his father got home from work, he tried in vain to talk his son into going back to school the next day, but he wouldn't. He was too proud.

"I swore no one would ever laugh at my English again, by God," he'd once told Holdorff. And no one ever did.

Tavisón joined the Marine Corps. The Second World War was coming to an end. The Germans were on the verge of surrender, and it seemed only a matter of weeks before Japan would be defeated, too. Tavisón was only sixteen, so he got his father and mother to lie about his age and went off to boot camp at Camp Pendleton. By the time he completed basic training, his English had improved greatly, but by then the Marines were more interested in his facility with Spanish.

After basic he was shipped to the Philippines and served as an interpreter for the duration of the war, which was getting near its end. V.E. Day had just happened. When the truce was signed at the end of summer ending

The Muttering Retreats

was signed at the end of summer ending the war in the Pacific, he stayed on for six months and then was shipped home and discharged at Camp Pendleton. He got out in January of 'forty-six, just in time to get enrolled at Long Beach City College which he attended for two years. He would have gone to Long Beach State after City, but it was January, and State wasn't due to open till September of 'forty-nine, so instead he chose to go to Los Angeles State which was just beginning its second academic year. He would be in the first graduating class from that college.

The barrio of East Los Angeles, not far from campus, was his first real encounter with Chicanos and the language they spoke, a strange bilingual mixture of Mexican-style Spanish and American English pidginized to the point that English words like "chair" came out "shair," and "short" came out "chort." Other English words like "car" became "carucha." He thought this would have been a better place for his parents to move to than Long Beach. He might have fit in better at Garfield or Roosevelt High than he had at Long Beach Poly.

While he attended Los Angeles State, he lived in an apartment in City Terrace, a mile down Eastern Avenue from campus. He supplemented his G.I. benefits as a bartender in a beer joint on Whittier Boulevard. He majored in history and minored in English.

Most of his friends at State were veterans like himself. They were generally older and more serious about their studies than the kids who'd just graduated from high school. Their chief concern was to get an education so that they could get good jobs. They weren't fraternity and athletic types. They'd go to a football game or two during the season, but they weren't interested in a lot of the other kid's stuff the fraternity boys were into. When they raised hell, they'd do it in the beer bars around town rather than in fraternity houses, and when it was time to study, they studied alone in their apartments or at the library.

During spring vacation of his senior year, Tavisón went to Long Beach to visit his parents, and while he was there, he made a call on the school district office to check out the job situation. To his surprise he was offered a position at his old alma mater to teach freshman history. Thus, he returned triumphantly, and speaking perfect American English, to Long Beach Polytechnic High School. He went back to State to finish his last semester of course work with a contract in hand.

The Muttering Retreats

With a great deal of pride, Tavisón graduated from college. His proud parents attended the graduation. By this time he was speaking English like a native-born American, and even though he spoke it like an educated person, he still maintained a certain middle class simplicity. He didn't want his erudition to seem phony or affected, and his teaching style reflected this desire. From his first day as a classroom teacher at Poly till the day he retired from City College, he maintained his just-another-one-of-the-guys strut when he lectured in front of the class. He wore a crew cut through periods that saw long-haired beats and hippies come and go. Because of his hairstyle, he was always being mistaken for a P.E. teacher.

"Hell no," he'd say, "I'm not one of those guys who throws a ball out to the class and spends the rest of the period in the coffee locker. I work for a living."

And that's exactly how he viewed teaching school. It was work, hard work at that.

During his first two years at Poly, he took classes three nights a week at the newly founded Long Beach State College, after which he got an M.A. degree in English and a junior college teaching credential. He went into English because, since graduating from Los Angeles

51

State, he'd wanted to develop a better understanding of poetry, learn more about it.

Tavisón got the job at City immediately upon receiving his M.A. degree. He was in his second year there when Holdorff showed up. He liked City better than Poly. He especially enjoyed his remedial English classes because, to him, working with the kids who couldn't read or write, or thought they couldn't read or write, was more like teaching than having literary and philosophical discussions with the bright kids in a 1A or 1B class. However, he did like to engage those high achievers out in the little English department quad. Indeed, Tavisón could hold his own in such discussions, and he certainly enjoyed getting into them, but he thought that showing a kid who would say, "I was never any good in English," how to write a simple, declarative sentence was really the essence of his job. It was with just such an attitude that he took Holdorff under his wing when he was in his remedial English class.

Unlike Tavisón, Holdorff had graduated from high school, but Holdorff didn't have Tavisón's kind of confidence in himself. That would come later as his general skepticism grew. Tavisón was an iconoclast, and Holdorff liked it because it reminded him of Rheinhardt. If some-

The Muttering Retreats

thing was ridiculous, Tavisón would say so. It was almost impossible for him to hurt anyone's feelings, because he would say it in such an inoffensive, logical, common sense way, which was also the way he conducted his classes. His honesty was flawless. You got the grade you deserved, and his approach to the language was so simplistic that if you didn't get it from him, you weren't going to get it.

Holdorff had taken all the requisite English classes in high school, but he didn't realize how little he'd gotten out of them until he got into Tavisón's class. All through high school, he'd been taught parts of speech and sentence structure by diagramming sentences. Tavisón simply did it by showing how sentences usually expressed action or state of being, and the subject was the word that came before the action, and the object came after it. He'd write a sentence on the blackboard and pace back and forth examining and identifying each word by underlining the subject once, the verb twice and the object three times. Constant repetition of this process assured even the slowest students of getting it.

Holdorff found all the repetition unnecessary, but not boring because he was so good at it. He took to language like birds take to flight.

He got A's on everything he did in remedial English. He was the best student in the class, and as for Tavisón's suggestion that he go into history, Holdorff just didn't want to do it. He thought history was just publicity for fame seekers. Take the wars out of history books, and there's nothing left. Tavisón had taken him from writing single paragraphs in the remedial class to full five-paragraph essays in 11A. The reading was more complex, too. From it he learned about Aristotelian logic, the dialectic and the syllogism.

He got into prose and poetry in English 1B. That was where he discovered "The Love Song of J. Alfred Prufrock." It's true he'd bought a copy of the poem that night when he was with Rheinhardt at City Lights Books, and he'd read it before he left Letterman, but he didn't really understand it until Tavisón discussed it in 1B. He was stunned by the starkness of Prufrock's alienation.

He'd entered a stage in his life where he began to write poetry seriously, and he was constantly after Tavisón for reading lists and recommendations of different poets. Holdorff was trying to make up for all the literature he'd missed in high school. For the first time in his life, he had a genuine interest in something he

54

thought worthwhile. He saw himself as a Beat poet, and he began cultivating that image. He let his hair and beard grow. At a time when his classmates were wearing short hair, he let his grow until it covered his ears and collar, and that proved to be a glaring contrast to his contemporaries' style, but he didn't care. He didn't have time to worry about something as mundane as personal appearance. He was too busy studying and writing poetry, and trying his hand at song lyrics as well. His beard, his long red hair and his pipe became his trademarks over the years. People from Long Beach to Santa Cruz and points in between would refer to them when they were trying to identify him to someone else.

As his interest in poetry and learning grew, his interest in academia waned so that by the time he graduated, he saw teaching and the college scene merely as a source of income to allow him to pursue comfortably the more important task of writing verse. Tavisón, and later Novak at State and Roget in Las Vegas, could see this metamorphosis and all they could do was encourage him. Tavisón gave up trying to get him into history. He knew where Holdorff's interest lay, and when he read some of his stuff, he had to agree that it wasn't bad poetry. In fact, his next self-chosen mentor at Long Beach State, Novak, thought it was so good that he told him about *Dust Books*, the directory of "little magazines," that forum in which aspiring poets and tellers of short tales could have their work published and get paid for it. The going rate for poetry was thirty copies, twenty for fiction.

Holdorff did eventually get published in one of the little magazines listed in *Dust Books,* an underground avant-garde publication called *Moondog*, current mostly at a few universities in the west. He'd submitted hundreds of poems to several different magazines (mainstream and underground) over the two years of his upper division college work, but he never gave up. The more he got rejected, the harder he worked at getting published. He was well aware of the accomplishment of the work stored in the re-frigerator, but that just wasn't good enough. Ul-timately, he wanted to get published. He thought his chances of being a popular songwriter were perhaps better than his chances of becoming a popular poet. Therefore, he'd write a piece that could go either way.

When First We Met

When first we met,

The Muttering Retreats

I wouldn't take a bet
That one day I'd fret
Over you.

But the more I got involved,
I somehow couldn't resolve
How you could revolve
'Round so many.

You told me from the start
You'd only break my heart,
But you didn't seem a tart,
So, I kept on.

Well, I wandered in
'Cause I wanted to begin
To know you and yer kin,
But I couldn't.

I just pushed on
Not seeing the con
That you'd put on
To get me.

Then the worst happened;
Love undampened
Took hold like a clamp and
We both fell.

Five

Holdorff took French in his first full-time semester at City, and it was in that class that he met the woman he'd marry and who'd bear his only child, a son. His marriage and subsequent divorce was one of the most grueling experiences of his life. It was about as tough as his tour of duty in the Navy. At no time before or after the Navy did he feel so helpless, so impotent, so powerless to do anything to control his own destiny. He didn't even feel that way now as his academic career seemed to be ending and he was about to leave Santa Cruz. He felt the least self-possessed during the less-than-two years that he was married.

His wife was an attractive young woman of Hawaiian ancestry who'd been a contestant in a beauty pageant in her senior year in high school. She was certainly well-endowed with those attributes that are required of beauty queens, but she didn't even make third runner-

The Muttering Retreats

up. That was the year before she met Holdorff. He was struck by her obvious beauty. She was a petite, dark-skinned flower of the islands with almond-shaped sloe-eyes. Born in Long Beach, she lived with her widowed mother who had migrated to the mainland with her husband when they were newlyweds. Holdorff's father-in-law had died in the war when his daughter was ten years old.

Holdorff was taken with her from the first time he saw her across the crowded classroom, but he didn't meet her face to face until almost a month later. One day as he was leaving campus and heading home, he saw her waiting at the bus stop. He pulled over to the curb and asked,

"Wan'a lift?"

Without a word, she got up from the bench and started for the car. He was surprised at how quickly she got into the Sedan Delivery. She had seemed so shy and reticent in class, and he really didn't think she'd recognize him, but to his surprise, she did recognize him as he'd pulled up, and *not* so surprisingly she was indeed shy. After he found out about her beauty pageant experience, he supposed it was her shyness that caused her to make such a poor showing. It certainly couldn't have been her obvious beauty.

"Mind if *I* smoke?" she asked, gesturing at his pipe.

"Nah. Go ahead," he replied.

She took a pack of Chesterfields and a book of matches out of her bag, shook out a cigarette and lit it. As she was doing this, he pulled over to the curb long enough to re-pack his pipe and get it started.

"So, yuh like the French class?" he asked.

"It's fun. And you?" She smiled agreeably.

"It's okay. Teacher's good, but I'm an English major, and I like my English class better. I got a really great teacher in that one."

"Oh? Who's that?"

"Tavisón."

"Ah, yes. I'm in his remedial English class."

"I had him for that last semester. Don't yuh think it's cool the way he paces in front of the blackboard? He struts like a hoodlum, and when he writes on the blackboard, it's like a little kid's scrawl."

"Yes, I've noticed. It's part of his charm. I think it's his way of relaxing you."

The Muttering Retreats

"Where yuh want me to drop yuh off?" he asked.

"I live on Gundry next to Mac Arthur Park, but if it's out of your way, you don't have to take me all the way home."

"No problem."

When they got to her place, she told him not to bother getting out of the car. She let herself out and walked to the front door where her mother was waiting. She had come out onto the stoop, curious to see who was dropping her daughter off. They both disappeared into the house without a backward glance.

The next day he talked to her briefly as they entered the classroom together. She, for all her shyness, sat in the second or third row in the middle. He usually sat a couple rows behind her by the window, a perfect vantage for looking at her profile. It was a beginning French class, and there were oral drills almost the whole period so he'd sneak peaks at her between drills. He took pleasure in watching her lithe, perfectly shaped contour.

He looked for her at the bus stop every day after that, but a couple weeks went by before he saw her there again. She was always right on time for the start of class, so he never got the chance to talk to her much then. Just when he was about to give up on the bus stop, she was there on a Friday. Her eyes had been on him from the moment he pulled out of the parking lot. She'd been as intent that day on finding him as he'd been on finding her. She batted her sloe-eyes, picked up her books and got into the car. She was just as reserved this time as she'd been before, so, while she smoked her Chesterfield, he puffed his pipe, turned the radio up and sang along with Hank Williams:

> Your cheatin' heart
> Will make you weep.
> You'll cry and cry
> And try to sleep.

He loved to sing along with the radio, even though he couldn't carry a tune. His singing was so bad that his voice went up or down an octave with each note. He sang along with songs he heard on the car radio, and he sang in the shower. He didn't have an ear for how bad it sounded, so he never really understood why people were so put off by it. It was another one of the supreme ironies of his life that he should love music so much and actually be a songwriter when he couldn't sing a lick.

The Muttering Retreats

"Hank's a great singer," he finally said. "Writes his own stuff, too."

"Yes," she replied, and said no more.

He didn't know what to make of her, whether she was just shy or whether she was subtly mocking him. Her silence made him uneasy. He started tapping the steering wheel with his fingers, trying to keep time with the music.

"I'd sure like to write that good," he finally said, no longer able to let the silence hang between them.

"Oh? You write?"

"I try."

"What do you write?"

"Poetry. I only just started when I was in the Navy. Met a guy when I was recuperating from my wound at Letterman up in Frisco. Name was Rheinhardt. Probably learned as much from him as I have from Tavisón. Started out just writing poetry, but now I'm tryin' to do song lyrics."

"Really."

And once again she stopped dead in her tracks. That went on for a couple minutes.

"How'd yuh like to go to a movie sometime?" he finally asked, though he wasn't sure why, since if he couldn't talk to her now, how the hell was he going to talk to her on a date?

"Fellini's latest, *La Strada*'s playing at the Bay in Seal Beach."

"When would you like to go?" she asked.

"How 'bout tonight?"

"That'd be fine. I don't have any plans."

"Terrific. Show starts at eight. How about I pick yuh up at six? We can get something to eat at Domenico's in the Shore before the movie, and after, we can go to the Forty Niners for a couple a' beers."

"Dinner and the movie will be fine, but I'm only nineteen."

"Not to worry. I know the bartender, and he won't ask yuh for I.D. if you're with me."

They drove the rest of the way to her house in silence, except his humming and singing with the music on the radio. As she was getting out of the car, her mother once again stepped out the front door, but this time she walked out to greet them. The daughter leaned back into the car and said,

"Here comes my mother."

He shut the engine off, got out and walked around to the sidewalk where they were standing. He shook hands with the mother, who wasn't as shy as her daughter. In fact, she was as gregarious as her daughter was reticent. As

The Muttering Retreats

time passed and he got to know her better, he would learn that she was outgoing to the point of obsequiousness. Holdorff figured the daughter must have gotten her shyness from her father.

"Well, I guess I'll see yuh tonight," he said, after the daughter told her mother about the date. "I'll be here at six. You got a phone?"

"Mm hmm."

"Can I have the number just in case?"

After writing it down, he got back into his car and drove off. That was the beginning of the end of Holdorff's bachelorhood.

They went to the movie that night, and afterward they went to the Forty Niners for a couple beers. As Holdorff had said, he knew the bartender, and he didn't check her I.D. This impressed her. Even though he was still only twenty-two, she thought of him as an "older man," more mature than the boys she'd gone out with in high school.

Things started happening fast after that. Holdorff found himself suffering extreme fits of jealousy when he'd see her walking around campus with other guys, but what he didn't know was that she was feeling the same kind of insecurity as he was. They both needed to relax and stop doubting each other, but they couldn't.

Jerome Arthur

Instead, they'd be alternately heart broken and suspicious of each other, and that put them on edge, and they'd bicker. These mixed feelings were fertile ground for Holdorff's writing. One of the times when he swore he was through with her, he wrote a couple songs:

Another Show

I took your honest word for it,
And I shouldn't 'a', I must admit.
It was only another show;
And now I'm laughin' as I go.

(Refrain)
Seems you were just jivin' me;
You did it so connivingly.
I really didn't want it anyhow,
And so I'm much better off now.

You did what I expected you to do;
I'm not surprised now that I'm so blue.
It ended before it ever got started,
And now I'm glad that we finally parted.
(Refrain)

I only wanted to be your friend,
But that turned out to be a dead end.
Friends don't leave friends alone
Waiting patiently by the telephone.
(Refrain)

66

The Muttering Retreats
Vicissitudes

I thought I'd found the ideal romance
When you said you could make love
Twice every day and Sunday.

So I set out on a journey to get
What I'd never had before now,
Only to find you resisting my love.

(Refrain)
What exactly do you mean
When you say what you say?
Whatever it is, it'll change in a day.

I no longer try to figure it out.
Your contradictions are too many,
And it's all way too confusing.
(Refrain)

When he finished the two songs, he put the originals on the stack in the icebox and the carbons in the wooden outbox he kept next the antique Underwood.

It was with exactly the feelings he'd expressed in those song lyrics that he took her to his bed the first time. She'd decided the relationship was no good and that she didn't want to see him anymore. Late one night as she was out cruising with one of her friends who had her father's car, she stopped in on him at his cottage and got him out of bed to tell him that it was over.

"I can't stay long," she said. "Sara brought me over and she's waiting in the car. I came by to tell you I want to break up."

"Wait. You can stay long enough to talk about it. Go tell Sara I'll take yuh home."

When she got back, he took a couple beers from the refrigerator and sat down with her.

"You can't break it off now," he said, getting up and going over to the box with the carbon copies. "I think I'm in love with you. Check this out."

He grabbed the carbon of a song he'd just completed that day. He handed it to her and she read, crying softly as she did so:

Already Been

You came into my life in such a subtle way.
I couldn't see what was happening to me,
But I hung on. It felt so good;
It felt as bad as I knew it would.

Chorus:
I already been
Where you're goin', my friend,
And I don't wan'a
Be there again.

68

The Muttering Retreats

You had your ways, and I had mine,
With so many miles between them.
We thought we knew it all.
How painful when we finally did fall.
Chorus:

The chance was a million to one.
We took it like we knew what to do.
You told me that I was the only one,
And I believed you didn't say it for fun.
Chorus:

"Oh, I love you, too, but I just don't feel right about this."

They went back and forth this way between guilt and innocence until finally he got her into his bed. And that was when everything changed. It was her first sexual experience, and she wasn't going to let him forget it. Thus, following her lead, he started to feel obligated to marry her. After he got her in the sack, that's all she talked about, and she talked more now than at any other time he could remember. During their early courtship, she talked very little. He'd rambled on about his studies and his writing while she listened quietly and admiringly, but after he bedded her, she paid little attention to what he had to say about some poet he was studying or a poem or song he might be working

69

on. When he finished telling her, she'd start talking about marriage and having babies. He couldn't see what was about to hit him. He was still enthralled by her sloe-eyed good looks, and her simple, deferential manner toward him.

They went through all the stages of romance. Once they discovered the sexual part of it, they did it all the time. It was the mid 'fifties; you had to go up to the counter and ask for "prophylactics." For the most part they weren't using anything. This contributed to their feelings of guilt, and it led to the second stage. Her talk of marriage and kids made him react by vowing to himself not to take her to bed again. But he couldn't keep his oath, so the cycle went on. For her part, she told him she couldn't go to bed with him anymore unless they got married. He really didn't want to get married at that time, but his heart throbbed for her. Holdorff began to feel trapped. He could see his options diminishing, but he still couldn't see what was happening.

The last stage of the romance began when she told him she was pregnant. One weekend in the fall, they drove to Las Vegas and were married by a justice of the peace in a quiet civil ceremony. When they returned, she moved into his cottage where they set up housekeeping.

The Muttering Retreats

That was the last time he sacrificed himself to respectability and appearances.

They both continued in school until the end of the semester, at which time she quit to become a housewife and to await the arrival of the baby. Holdorff continued on in school in more of a hurry now than ever. He was beginning to feel the pressure of the family man's responsibility. Now his goal was to finish school as soon as possible so that he could get a job. He started his junior year at State in the spring semester. The baby was born in summer. It was a boy and Holdorff got to name him. He chose Humphrey after his favorite movie actor, Humphrey Bogart. He called the boy H.H. after Hunter Hancock, a rhythm and blues deejay he liked, who broadcast out of a radio station in South Central Los Angeles.

After H.H. was born, his mother became a social invalid. Suddenly, she seemed unable to function without her mother. When the baby was born, mother and child went to her mother's house from the hospital. They stayed there for almost a month before going home to Holdorff's cottage. He was feeling marginalized as a parent.

Holdorff could see that they had to find a bigger place to live. He wanted to move as far away as possible from her mother, but she wanted to move closer. They eventually got a two-bedroom apartment a half-mile away. Everyday when he got home from his after-school job at the A & P, he either found his gregarious mother-in-law at his house, or his wife was at her mother's. On days when the former was the case, he would listen to their chatter for about five minutes and then remove himself to the Forty Niners for a few beers. He actually liked the other days because he could sit down and write a poem or two in peace and quiet before he'd have to go pick up his family, but it was annoying coming home to an empty house, and after all, who was he married to anyway, her or her mother?

The marriage went like that until Humphrey was almost a year old, and then Holdorff gave up. One night he came home from the Forty Niners after her mother had left and dinner wasn't started. She asked him to go to the store and pick up some T.V. dinners. He wasn't quite drunk, but close. He got into an argument with her. After a few words were exchanged, he stalked out of the house, went back to the Forty Niners and didn't leave the joint until just before midnight. When he got home, she started in on him again, nagging him about his drinking and

The Muttering Retreats

about his not being polite to her mother and about anything else she could think of. It wasn't unusual for her to be up that late. Some nights she'd stay up watching the all night movies on T.V. and smoking cigarettes. He was tired and wanted to sleep, so he went to bed but couldn't get any shuteye because she had the T.V. turned up. He got out of bed and tramped out of the house and slept in the back of his car.

"I think I'm go'n'a talk to my old landlord, see if I can move back into my cottage," he told her the next morning. "This marriage thing just isn't workin' for me. You maybe ought'a take the baby and move back home with your mother. You seem to wan'a spend more time with her than me."

He had to admit that his heart no longer throbbed for her, and he actually didn't care if he ever saw her again. He remembered how his heart used to ache at the mere thought of her. Now it was a matter of survival. He suddenly realized that he didn't have time for heartache. He was going to school full-time and pushing produce part-time at the A & P, and she couldn't even have dinner on the table when he got home because she was hanging with her mother. He'd had it.

"I don't want the marriage to end," she said. "Can't we talk about this?"

"I'm done talking. I don't think we can resolve anything."

He left for school on that note. At the end of the day, and after a few beers at the Forty Niners, he went home and told her he hadn't changed his mind. He wanted to move out. She pouted as he told her this, and then she begged him not to go, that she'd change, that they should see a marriage counselor, all to no avail. His mind was made up. He'd had enough, and he didn't want to take the chance of falling into the same old pattern.

When she realized he wasn't going to change his mind, she went to the telephone, called her mother and told her to come pick her up. The mother asked to speak to Holdorff, and when he got on the line, she cursed him roundly, telling him that he ought to be ashamed of himself for deserting a young wife and helpless baby. But it had little impact on him; in fact, it only strengthened his resolve. When he gave the phone back to his wife, his mother-in-law's voice still rang in his ear. The tone was indignant, but the purpose was to cajole, and Holdorff knew it, could feel it.

The Muttering Retreats

When his wife got back on the phone, he went over to his son's playpen (the boy was still awake at that late hour) and picked him up to talk to him and reassure him. He was only a one-year-old baby, and Holdorff wanted more than anything not to make him feel insecure. It was bad enough that everybody else was so upset. No use upsetting the child, too. Just as Holdorff was hugging and comforting him before going out the door, his wife, having just hung up the phone, came over and snatched the baby out of his arms as though she were afraid he was going to harm him in some way. He reacted by reaching out and slapping her across the face. He did it before he could stop himself. It was a reflex action, prompted by fear. The woman was hitting him on two fronts, or that's how he saw it anyway. She was depriving him of H.H.'s affections and actually accusing Holdorff of wanting to harm the boy.

"He's my baby too, you know," he said, immediately sorry for slapping her. She looked at him with hatred in her eyes.

"Get out!" she hissed, holding the baby away from him.

Any composure Humphrey might have had was gone. He bawled and shrieked, more shaken than scared, and Holdorff felt awful. His cocksure green eyes framed in tiger-striped plastic dissolved into misty sorrow, his bearded cheeks quivered. He turned and headed for the door.

They'd had a beautiful love affair that ended the day they got married. He thought she'd put him through the wringer during the marriage, but then he was sure she thought the same about him. It was a critical time for him because it was happening right when he was starting his senior year at State. It was rough for him anyway without her making it worse. He completed his senior year and graduated, but the ending of his marriage didn't make it easy for him during that time.

One of the better things to come from the split was that now he had a good subject to write about. So, between drinking bouts, he couldn't write it down fast enough. He came home one night after a few beers at the Forty Niners and cranked out seven new poems. The one he liked best of the seven was something he called "Five Quartets":

> I guess there's no getting' over it—
> When your lover's lovin' someone new,
> You just can't seem to get used to it,
> No matter what you do.

The Muttering Retreats

When first you get the word,
Your anger only wants to shout,
But you find you just can't feel that way
And claim to know what it's all about.

Now it's your turn to hurt,
And you feel like it'll never end,
But you've just got to hang on
If you ever want to love again.

Soon enough you'll accept it.
It's all you can do to keep on,
Knowing that you're not special,
Just another body to lean on.

So if you look for refuge
From family, friends and home,
It's only natural that you would,
So you won't feel so all alone.

He'd forged ahead, but he started drinking heavily during the separation and divorce, and it continued through his last year in college. He drank himself into a stupor four or five nights a week, which began to show in his physical appearance. He got bloated and his green eyes seemed to relinquish their sparkle to a drunken glaze. Amazingly, it didn't affect his schoolwork significantly. He seemed to thrive on the emotional pressure he was under.

Jerome Arthur

Just because he was now divorced didn't mean that the confrontations with his ex-wife and her mother ended. After a blowout he'd typically go to the Forty Niners and have a few beers. Then he'd go home and write a poem about the experience. As he'd done so many times before, he'd walk to the refrigerator, grab a beer, stand in front of the still-open door, sip the beer and read his poem. When he finished reading, he'd separate the original from the carbon, place the original on top of a stack of other white sheets inside the empty refrigerator, empty except for a half-gone six-pack box of Budweiser bar bottles, and then place the carbon in the outbox. Afterward he'd sit at the counter puffing on his pipe until his bottle was empty. Leaving the bottle on the counter, he'd get to his feet and go to bed. On the days when he'd close the Forty Niners, he wouldn't make it home until after two in the morning, in which case he'd flop down on his bed without writing a poem, without undressing and without even brushing his teeth.

He was unable to get his old cottage when his wife moved back to her mother's house, but he got a single apartment about twenty yards from the beach on the ocean side of the Belmont Peninsula. To call it an apartment was an overstatement. The space was about ten by fourteen feet at the back of a small two-car garage. It was furnished with a loveseat-size foldout davenport on one wall and a twin bed along the opposite wall. Holdorff had built bookshelves on brackets above the couch. There was also a counter with a hot plate, a small refrigerator and a sink. His toilet and shower were in a small lean-to off to the side.

After he'd gone to court and gotten an interlocutory decree, he was ordered to pay child support, which he was already paying, and granted "reasonable visitation rights." The first weekend he called to pick H.H. up, his ex-wife said he could come to her house and visit with his son there, but he couldn't take him anywhere. That was her idea of "reasonable visitation rights," but not his, so he said he'd talk to his lawyer. The Legal Aid lawyer said he'd take care of it, and that evening when Holdorff got home, his ex-wife called and told him to come the following Sunday and pick the boy up. He didn't know what the attorney had done, but whatever it was, it worked, and from that time until he moved to Las Vegas, he picked H.H. up every Sunday around noon and took him back to his mother in the evening. They went to the park, the Pike, and sometimes they'd go back to

Holdorff's cottage and hang around at the beach. The apartment was barely big enough for him alone, so it was definitely too small for the two of them.

After the split and subsequent visitation battle, he immersed himself in his writing. This was the period in his life when he learned the most about technique, the mechanics of poetry. He studied the French symbolists and the Americans of the nineteen-twenties, and then he'd try to imitate them. He was writing poems that took the shape of fountains and downtown buildings, the surf and the clouds that drifted overhead, and all of the originals went onto the stack that kept the beer company on the refrigerator shelf. The carbons went into the outbox, and were later sent out for publication.

The same went for the songs he wrote. At the time the main difference between his songs and his poems was content. Holdorff developed a keen interest in the latest popular music format: rock 'n' roll, and its predecessor rhythm and blues. He especially liked the work of Jerry Leiber and Mike Stoller. He knew that Jerry wrote the lyrics and Mike wrote the music. They were writing hit after hit for various Atlantic Records recording artists. One of his songs

The Muttering Retreats

that he thought was just as good as anything
they wrote was titled "Shut Down."

Ain't it just like life
To sneak up on you
When you ain't ready,
Only to tell you:

(Refrain)
Shut down
Run out of town
Shoved into the
Underground.

Got'a force yo'self
To keep on trying'
To keep from cryin'
And not let it be:
(Refrain)

Yo' friends'll change.
They ain't the same,
But you can't let 'em
Put you down and say:
(Refrain)

You'll ask yo'self
Why it's happenin',
And you don't get
But one answer:
(Refrain)

Jerome Arthur

If only he could find someone like Mike Stoller to write some music for his lyrics. He pictured them accompanied by electric guitar, bass, drums and maybe even a boogie-woogie piano. But until he could get it accepted for publication, he'd have to settle for putting it on the stack in the refrigerator, and whenever he moved, he'd tie what was loose into a bundle so that after a few moves, he had a stack of bundles with some loose papers on top.

Six

Holdorff took American lit. (Civil War to present) in his first semester at State, right around the same time as he was splitting up with his wife. The teacher's name was Novak, and he was a real taskmaster. His discipline reminded Holdorff of some of the Marine drill instructors he'd had when he was learning the manual of arms in Navy boot camp. Novak was especially hard on the women in the class, and also outwardly indifferent to them, which to Holdorff seemed ironic because those same women tended to be in awe of him. Novak had a little-tough-guy Bogart/Cagney air about him. A cigar chomping Edward G. Robinson, he was never "on the make." He didn't have to be. The ladies seemed to flock around him as they often do with certain outlaw types.

Within the first two weeks of his being in Novak's class, Holdorff found out just how tough he was. As he'd done everyday since the start of the semester, Novak sat at the table in front of the class chomping the two-inch butt of his stogie. The students had been assigned the John Greenleaf Whittier poem "Skipper Ireson's Ride." When Novak started the discussion, he asked the class what the references in the first stanza were about—"Apuleius's Golden Ass" and "Islam's prophet on Al-Borák." As he asked the question, he stood up and walked over to the window. As though he were aiming it at someone down below, he tossed the cigar butt out the second-storey window. Then he turned back to the blank stares of the class and repeated the question. No one could give him the answer, so he sent the entire class to the library.

Holdorff remembered Apuleius from the world lit. class he'd taken from Powers at City, but he couldn't remember the specifics, so he went to the card file and found *Writers of the Western World*, the anthology used in Powers' class, the same anthology Rheinhardt had carried around at Letterman. He got the answer to the Al-Borák question from the dictionary. At about twenty minutes past the hour, he was the first one to get back to class.

"So, what'd you find out, Mister Holdorff?" Novak asked.

The Muttering Retreats

"Apuleius was an African writer during the Roman times. About one-sixty A. D. He wrote a collection of stories in Latin called *The Golden Ass* or the *Metamorphoses.* Al-Borák was the white, winged creature that took Mohammed to the seventh heaven."

"Good. Now let's see if anybody else got it."

By ten-thirty about half the class had returned so Novak resumed the discussion. When the class ended at ten till, only about two-thirds were present. Novak questioned all of them individually and in groups as they got back to the classroom.

"Let this be a lesson. Don't even come to class if you're not prepared. Now, get outa' here. I'll see you Friday."

Despite his exacting approach to literature and his tough-guy demeanor, Novak was very entertaining in the classroom, always a lot of laughs. The other classes going on in the building could hear the laughter. In some ways he was a frustrated stand-up comic, breezing along, acting his way through all of his classes, having a guaranteed audience who laughed at his jokes. Of all the people whom Holdorff had met and would meet in his campus travels, Novak was the most comfortable in his own skin; his was the most relaxed existence of them all.

However, Holdorff found that Novak was precious little help to him when it came to his personal problems. He was a great classroom teacher, but he knew very little about personal relationships. He'd never been married, much less been through a divorce, so he had little first-hand experience with such matters. He was caught between two personalities, a hard-nosed American lit. teacher in the classroom, a debonair gentleman outside of it, his sense of humor all that overlapped the two. All he knew about women was how to get them into the sack and then sweet-talk them out of his life after the conquest. He only made Holdorff feel inadequate in that regard.

Holdorff took Novak's American Novel class in his last semester at State, the fall semester. By then he'd gotten as tight with Novak as he'd been with Rheinhardt and Tavisón in the earlier stages of his education. The Novel class was only the second one Holdorff had taken with Novak, but he'd gotten really tight with him in the American lit. class, and they'd stayed close through the two semesters and two summers since.

The Muttering Retreats

One Friday afternoon in early December, when Novak was shopping at the A & P, he went to the produce counter to say hello to Holdorff who was just getting ready to punch out at the end of his shift.

"Wan'a go across the street for a drink?" Novak asked.

"Hoefly's?"

"Where else? You know you're not go'n'a catch me in any of the beer joints you hang around in."

Hoefly's was a swanky little club with red carpets and valet parking. Kelly's and Jack's Corsican Room, both in Naples, were the only other two bars in the Shore that Novak would go to.

"Sure," Holdorff said.

He'd gone to Hoefly's with Novak before, and when he did, he ordered a Heineken. Why not? Novak picked up the tab. It was one of the few times when Holdorff could indulge himself. He thought it might be nice to go to a joint like Hoefly's more often, but that was probably not in the cards for him. He couldn't afford places like Hoefly's. He could barely afford a place like the Forty Niners. He had responsibilities now, and he needed to rethink his priorities. H.H. was now two years old and with

87

each passing year would require more attention, both emotionally and financially. So Holdorff would simply have to stick with Coors or Oly on tap, and have Heineken only when Novak invited him to Hoefly's.

"You know, Doctor Novak," Holdorff said as they sat at the bar. "They're talking about you in class. Some of the girls are saying you got something going on with that cute little brunette sitting in the front row by the window."

"Oh, yeah? What're they saying?"

"Passed a couple gals going into class this morning, and overheard 'em saying your name and the girl's name, and then they both giggled to beat hell. Couldn't make out exactly what they said, but I can imagine."

"Really? What can they possibly think we're doing?"

There was a facetious note in Novak's tone.

"All I know is I see you two together a lot around campus. You've got'a be careful. You could get your ass booted outa' there."

"Yeah, well, I'll try to exercise a little more discretion."

Novak sounded flip.

The Muttering Retreats

"How do you do it, anyway? I was never any good at that. Been a year since I split with my wife, and haven't had any luck at all."

"I really don't know. They just seem to come to me."

There were a few couples at tables in the lounge waiting to be seated in the dining room. A man and a woman sat together at one end of the bar when Holdorff and Novak came in. Shortly after the two guys took their stools at the other end, the couple picked up and went into the dining room, and just then an attractive blond woman came in and sat by herself a few stools away. She was dressed for an evening on the town, high heels, a slinky cocktail dress, and a chinchilla wrap. She looked to be in her early to mid thirties. Holdorff and Novak were positioned so that they faced each other, thus giving Novak a view of her over Holdorff's shoulder. When she'd finished about half of her cocktail, Novak called the bartender over and told him to set her up with a fresh drink. As the bartender set the drink in front of her, he said,

"This one's on the gentleman at the end of the bar, ma'am."

When she looked their way, she saw a smiling Novak holding his glass up in front of him, toasting her. She smiled back and took a sip from her fresh drink.

"You're unbelievable. You know that?" Holdorff said as he turned back and faced Novak.

"Will you take a look at her," Novak said in a low voice. "What a knockout!"

Holdorff turned back around and took another look. He had to admit, she was beautiful. Her cosmopolitan demeanor gave her that extra dimension beyond mere physical beauty. She had class and she exuded it all over the place.

"Guess this is where I came in," Holdorff said. "Go'n'a finish my beer and hit the road."

In fact, he was beginning to feel out of place in that elegant setting that was filling up with diners dressed to the nines. He was aware that he didn't fit in with his long hair, full beard and rumpled corduroy sports jacket with leather patches on the elbows.

"Suit yourself," said Novak. "I think I'll move down the bar and join the lady."

Holdorff finished his beer, thanked Novak for buying it for him and headed out. As he passed the blond, he smiled at her and she

90

The Muttering Retreats

smiled back. He gave the lounge one last look as he left. Novak was moving in on the blond.

He went to the Forty Niners where he spent the better part of the evening drinking draft beer and engaging in philosophical and literary discussions with the various barroom philosophers, mostly students and at least one teacher. At midnight he found himself alone at the bar, the bartender the only other person in the place. He killed off his beer and left. When he crossed the Davis Bridge into Naples on his way home, he decided to take a run down Second Street to see if anything was happening in any of the beer joints there.

He stopped in front of a place he'd been to a couple times called the Acapulco Inn. Like the Forty Niners, the A.I. was a college bar. It was long and narrow with a fireplace in the center and a room in back with a ping-pong table. The only other people in the joint were the bartender and four guys in the ping-pong room. They weren't playing. They were filling their glasses from a pitcher, toasting each other and talking about a trip two of them had been on in late summer and early fall. They'd only gotten back a couple weeks ago. Holdorff ordered a draft and sat down by the fire. He couldn't help overhearing the conversation in the ping-pong room. One of the guys was saying, "…sailed to the Marquesas first…then on to Tahiti, Fiji and Phoenix Island…came home from Honolulu…cool trip…."

"Hear, hear. To a cool trip," said another, holding up his beer mug.

All four of them were feeling no pain. The two guys had sailed on a thirty-five foot Tahiti ketch. For one of them, it had been his second trip to the south Pacific. The two who hadn't gone were awe struck, listening to how it had been. They were all young, about Holdorff's age.

Holdorff was suddenly aware that he was very tired, so he drank his beer down and got off the bar stool. That's when he realized how drunk he was. He felt light-headed, and his knees buckled momentarily. When he got his balance, he walked out into the cool, briny air.

He took a walk around the block before getting into his car. He knew his own limits. He was too drunk to just get behind the wheel and drive home. Luckily he didn't have far to go, only down to Sixty-ninth Place on the Peninsula. As he drove down Ocean Boulevard, he slowed when he got to Fifty-fourth Place. He could see Novak's red Jaguar parked in the carport next to his building at the corner of Bay-

The Muttering Retreats

shore Walk where his second-storey apartment looked out on Alamitos Bay. He wondered if the woman he'd seen earlier in Hoefly's was still with Novak.

He got home without incident and went straight to his typewriter. He took a cancelled envelope from his jacket pocket and spent five minutes trying to concentrate on some of the things he'd experienced that night, but couldn't. His thoughts were confused, his words gibberish. He walked over to the refrigerator and discovered that he was out of beer. That was okay. He really didn't need another beer. He reached for the top sheet on the stack. It was a song he'd written the night before, and at the time, it sounded pretty good, but now it seemed blurred.

Goodbye for Good

When you said goodbye for good,
You told me I was too intense,
But I didn't think you would,
Believing you had confidence
That our relationship withstood
Even that consequence.

(Chorus)
So, where do I go from here?
I do believe the end is near.
Maybe I'll see you again,

93

But neither of us knows when.

You warned me many a time
That my own intensity
Only made you want to climb
Into your own immensity.
Seems all we did was pantomime
The way to our destiny.
(Chorus)

All that's left is the torment
That my intensity repulsed
You when it was really meant
To achieve the opposite results.
Ah, if we'd only bent,
We'd just now be starting to exult.
(Chorus)

Now the pain it just begins
As everything else ends.
I know I'll never convince
You to stay and make amends.
I do so hope to see that glint
In your eyes again.
(Chorus)

He was acutely aware of how confused
his thoughts were, so he finally just gave it up
and went to bed.

Seven

Holdorff got his B.A. degree in January and took a midterm-teaching job at Jordan High in North Long Beach. During his one semester at Jordan, he got accepted in the M.A. program at the Southern Division of the University of Nevada in Las Vegas. He had packed his gear and moved to the desert one week after H.H.'s third birthday. Leaving the boy was the hardest part of the move. He vowed to make frequent weekend trips to Long Beach to visit him.

In his first semester at S.D.U.N., Holdorff took a graduate seminar in twentieth century American poetry from a guy named Roget, and he liked him and the class immediately. Roget's teaching style was a lot like Novak's. He conducted the class as if it were a platoon of raw recruits, and he were their master sergeant. They were also both small guys, but that's where the similarities ended. Whereas Novak was a well-tailored, well-barbered lady's man,

Roget was the consummate rumpled, intellectual schoolteacher who wouldn't be caught dead in a barbershop. His wife cut his hair in the bright glare of the ceiling light in the kitchen. He had little time to worry about his physical appearance; he was too busy writing, teaching and thinking about subjects as diverse as baseball and classic cars.

In his second semester, Holdorff took an upper division Modern Drama class from Roget. They started with Henrik Ibsen and ended with Arthur Miller. Roget ran an especially tight ship in the big classes like Modern Drama, but he was also very strict in the small graduate seminars.

He'd march in, set his briefcase next to the podium on the table, remove the podium and stand it on its side on the floor in the corner. Then he'd reach into the briefcase, pull out the anthology for the class, five manila folders stuffed with notes and papers, and stack all of it neatly on the table (Holdorff couldn't say he'd ever seen Roget open the folders and look at any of the notes or papers in them). He set the briefcase against the wall behind his chair. The last detail was to bring the waste paper basket over next to his chair so that he could tap the burned tobacco from his pipe into it before reloading.

The Muttering Retreats

After he sat down, he'd open the top folder, which had a seating chart and roll sheet, and take the roll. Whichever seat you took on the first day of class was your seat, and if you weren't in it when he took roll, you were marked absent, and if you were absent three times, he'd call you up to his desk to warn you that if you were absent one more time, he'd drop you from the class.

The first time he called Holdorff's name in the poetry seminar, he said "Holdoff," and Holdorff corrected him. One of the students, Rierson, pronounced with a long "i," didn't correct Roget when he mispronounced it "Rearson" until about three quarters of the way through the semester, but then it was too late. Roget had "Rearson" in his head, and that's the way Rierson would be known henceforth in Roget's class. After he took the roll, he started the class with,

"What's this play about?"

Roget almost never lectured, even with the larger classes. Rather he'd sit at the table conducting discussions, dropping ash from his pipe into the wastebasket, then repacking it with fresh tobacco. He was sure to hit everybody with at least one question, so you better, by God, be prepared when you came to *his* class.

The only time he lectured was when a specific subject that interested him came up in the course of a discussion. Holdorff didn't mind that Roget was so hardnosed. It reminded him of Novak, and he needed the discipline, anyway.

Roget's Modern Drama class was Holdorff's second shot at the subject, and he got into it in a big way. His first attempt was a class at Long Beach City called Introduction to Theater Arts, but that was a straight drama class. Roget's was a lit. class, and that's one of the reasons Holdorff took to it so enthusiastically. Another reason was Roget's knowledge of the subject. Of the many different hats Roget wore at S.D.U.N., his favorite was being a playwright. He loved to write dialogue. He had a dozen or so finished manuscripts to his credit, and he'd even had a couple of the plays produced at the studio theater on campus. Roget started working on a new play, his first musical, at the beginning of spring semester. He asked Holdorff and another grad. student in the class, a piano playing music major named Eliot, to write the words and music to the songs.

At first Holdorff thought he was finally going to get a chance to stretch his song writing skills, but as time passed and he got into the project, he was discovering that the format just didn't suit him. He was really more interested in writing rock 'n' roll lyrics. But he forged ahead, thinking it was good that he was finally working with a real musician. And Eliot was that if he was anything. He was a classically trained pianist who could play anything: blues, boogie-woogie, honky tonk, but especially classical. Over time, Roget couldn't get into the groove that Eliot, Holdorff and Baldwin, the choreographer, were in. Roget was too literary, not musical.

As Holdorff's knowledge of literature broadened, he would get argumentative with his teachers in class, but since he hadn't studied much drama and didn't think of himself as well-versed in the subject, he listened quietly in the Modern Drama class (probably for the first time since Tavisón) as Roget and the other students discussed the plays of Ibsen and Strindberg and Brecht. Holdorff only interjected comments when Roget put questions directly to him, and then Roget would wait apprehensively for the kind of argument Holdorff had given him in the poetry class. But it didn't happen.

Holdorff was a model student in the Modern Drama class, listening patiently and even taking notes occasionally when somebody said something significant. He was the oldest graduate student enrolled in S.D.U.N.'s English department, and that made him the oldest person in Roget's class. He found himself cast in the role of elder statesman. He and Eliot were the only graduate students in a class of upper-division under-graduates. At first, even the professors in the department treated him differently than they treated most of the other graduate students; however, that changed in a hurry. The undergraduates looked up to him, even though he was really just another lackey of a teaching assistant, hustling grades and reading blue books for a couple professors.

There was a lot of professional jealousy of Roget from among his English department colleagues. Of all of them, he was the most prolific writer, and his stuff was stuff he enjoyed writing, not the obligatory publish-or-perish tripe that his colleagues were shackled with. They couldn't seem to break away from their research long enough to do anything creative, so the next best thing was to be resentful of Roget. When Holdorff asked him to be his graduate adviser and chair his committee, Roget warned him about the risk he was taking.

"You know," he said, "you might jeopardize your chances by having me as your advisor."

The Muttering Retreats

"I'm not worried about it. I'll write a good thesis, and besides, I can B.S. with the best of 'em."

"I know, but sometimes it takes more than just bullshitting. Some of these guys take themselves far too seriously. Buncha' control nuts. They'll dump on you just for the hell of it. And if your name is associated with mine, it could hurt you more than help you."

Holdorff moved on indomitably, taking the required classes to complete his course work, preparing for his orals and comprehensives, and gathering research to use for his thesis, which he was sure by the time he'd asked Roget to be his advisor, would be on Allen Ginsberg.

The decade was coming to an end, and Holdorff felt it was high time that the Beats got recognized for their contribution to American literature. So he set out to spread their message in the halls of academia, not fully aware when he started out just exactly how much ahead of everybody else he really was. In five years time poets like Ginsberg and Lawrence Ferlinghetti and novelists like Jack Kerouac (he'd already hit the mainstream) and William Burroughs would be widely read on college campuses from coast to coast. The nineteen-sixties campus radi-

101

cals would, in fact, rally around them, singing their praises, even as Kerouac rebuked them as unpatriotic draft resisters.

When Holdorff was doing research for his thesis, the Beats's stock was so low that he ran into trouble finding information in the library. It also worked to his detriment in the same way selecting Roget to chair his committee had. The other members of the committee didn't consider the Beats legitimate writers. Those professors took to heart the Truman Capote comment about Kerouac not writing, but typing.

His inability to get adequate information marked the beginning of deteriorating relations between him and his committee, except for Roget, who didn't care if he finished the work or not. He would pass him, regardless. In fact, Roget would have handed Holdorff his M.A. outright. He thought he was just as qualified as some of his jealous colleagues in the English department, and they had Ph.D. degrees.

While he was working on the play, Holdorff spent a couple of hours every afternoon with Eliot at the piano after they'd read the pages Roget had written the night before. His songwriting career was hitting its stride as his time as a graduate student at S.D.U.N. was end-

The Muttering Retreats

ing. He became so immersed in the play that his studies went by the wayside. As he fell further behind in his classes and on his thesis, he noticed a subtle change in attitude coming from his other teachers. He could plainly see what Roget had been talking about in early spring when Holdorff asked him to be on his committee.

Those other teachers weren't the only ones whose attitudes were changing. Roget was changing, too. The more they worked together, the less they got along. Eliot and Baldwin stayed out of their bickering. They couldn't seem to agree on anything. Holdorff thought the songs should be light and lyrical; Roget didn't see his musical as all light comedy. The story was about a girl who has to break up with her boyfriend because her parents don't approve of him, and he can't get her out of his head. The boyfriend thinks she dumped him. He doesn't know her parents are behind it, so he sings a song, "Still on my Mind," about how "she done him wrong."

> She's still on my mind,
> Though she shouldn't be
> 'Cause how she treated me
> was so very unkind.
>
> (Refrain)

103

It's hard to believe
She'd ever leave.
I was out of tune
When she left so soon.

I'd do it all again
If I had the chance.
I'd at least learn to dance,
And she'd still be my friend.
(Refrain)

Eliot wrote some good music for that little ditty; he made it a blues number. Holdorff thought it sounded pretty good, but Roget wasn't happy with it. He didn't complain about the music; it was the lyrics he didn't like.

When the play was produced in the summer, this difference of opinion turned it into an artistic, critical and box office failure. Holdorff and Roget both would agree, when it was all over, that the play was no *Carousel*.

And so, Holdorff tried to salvage what was left of the spring semester. By mid May, they finished working on the musical, and he made up his mind to stay in Las Vegas through the summer to see it produced. Since he wouldn't be getting paid for the T.A.-ship in summer, he thought it would be a good idea to get a part-time job to supplement his Navy dis-

The Muttering Retreats

ability and G.I. bill. He went looking for work as a blackjack dealer in one of the downtown casinos. The one thing that bothered him about this plan was that he would be too busy to travel to Long Beach and connect with H.H. Holdorff didn't know when he'd be able to see him again. He'd called on the phone and spoken to the boy a few times over the nine months he'd been in the desert, and was acutely aware of how seldom that had been, which made him feel guilty, but he knew he couldn't dwell on it.

As the semester was winding down, Holdorff could see the handwriting on the wall. He was becoming a persona non grata at the university, but he figured he had no better place to go, so he made his intentions known that he'd like to return for the fall semester.

They finished writing the musical and began the production process in mid June. Roget procured the studio theater for three weekends in August. He cast and blocked the play in June and rehearsed it in July. Roget was never happy with the finished product, but Holdorff told him to relax, it was a good play, and it would be a big hit when it was performed. He lied. It did play to an almost sold-out house on opening night, but when the reviews came out, the box office died. On the second night, the theater was

105

only about half full, and the second and third weekends it played to an almost empty house. By then he and Roget weren't speaking to each other, and it was a good thing for Holdorff that school was out because all the other committee members were out of town, thus missing the disaster of the production, and even more important, missing the feud going on between the two writers.

"I'm so pissed off at you!" Roget said. "If they were in town, I'd go tell them what kind of a horse's ass you really are."

"Ah, come on, Roget. Get off my ass." Holdorff said. His face was calm, but his words were agitated. He lit his pipe between words and puffed smoke out his nose. "You wrote the goddamn play. It was your idea. All I did was help you out with a few song lyrics. And that was some damn good poetry, too. I can't help it you wanted to get serious with a musical comedy."

He might as well have been talking to the wall. Roget wasn't listening. All he could think of was the disaster of the failed production, and he was looking for someone to blame. Holdorff didn't even attend all the performances.

Things took a turn for the worse when school started in September. Holdorff was back

The Muttering Retreats

on good terms with Roget, but Roget wasn't teaching anything he could use. He'd given up his T.A.-ship because he'd gotten the blackjack job at the Pioneer Club. This made him more of an outcast than ever on campus. And if that wasn't bad enough, one of his committee members, a harsh critic of Roget, a bitter enemy, was teaching a class he needed. He was the only other American lit. scholar on the committee, and his dislike of Roget carried over to Holdorff. They started arguing on the first day of class, so Holdorff started thinking seriously about what he was going to do and where he was going to go next.

Eight

Holdorff went looking for a dealing job a week after the semester ended. He'd been intrigued by the possibility of being a dealer from the moment he'd arrived in Las Vegas, and he carried the thought around through the school year.

The university was new when Holdorff got accepted. It's true it had been going now for six years, but this was the first year that they had classes on their new campus. Heretofore, they'd been holding classes at Las Vegas High School. It was a small school in a small city. Enrollments were low and growing slowly. When he got there and saw the town, he thought he knew why. He figured it was a combination of the hot desert weather and the cheap, tawdry nature of the casino/hotel environment. That was Holdorff's impression from the beginning. As far as everybody else who lived there for any length of time and swore by it was concerned,

The Muttering Retreats

Las Vegas was an oasis that blossomed in a dry and barren land. He was astonished at how the inhabitants could still be awestruck by the neon on Fremont Street at midnight, even after seeing it for many years.

And their cool efficiency was as intense as the desert heat. Just being there and dealing with them, even Holdorff developed a modicum of efficiency, and that proved to be a good thing when it came to his studies. There was even an efficiency in the way the residents called the place "Vegas," as though they didn't want to waste any breath on extra syllables. Nobody seemed to want to make eye contact, not the bartenders, not the dealers, not the women who collected the cash at restaurants, not even the porter in the men's room. They all kept a low profile, trained to be aloof and remote.

When he decided to get a dealing job, he went to the casinos downtown and along the Strip, wandering around, looking things over. He'd only tried his hand at the tables a couple times in the nine months he'd been in town, so he really didn't know the scene. He preferred downtown to the Strip, and he had the feeling that's where he was eventually going to work, but he went out to the Strip anyway just to check it out.

Jerome Arthur

The Strip was just beginning to develop at that time. People had only recently started calling Las Vegas Boulevard by that name. It had only been ten years since the Flamingo was built. The Stardust was the latest attraction out there; it had just opened that spring. Holdorff decided to begin there. He sat down at a table with two other players, a beautiful young black woman and a haggard-looking middle aged tourist. The dealer's nametag said "Blake." She was a wholesome-looking, but petite blue-eyed woman with long blond hair. Holdorff had ten one-dollar chips and promptly lost five of them after five hands. Then his luck changed. He won a few hands, and the next thing he knew he was up twenty dollars, all the while having a good time with the dealer. She was taking pleasure in his beating the house.

"You seem to like your job," he said. "'Least you're havin' a good time right now."

"Not bad."

He still wasn't used to the abruptness. He was glad she softened it with a smile.

"Pay pretty good, does it?" he asked, holding a match over his pipe.

"Depends on the table. The bigger the play, the better you do."

The Muttering Retreats

She was friendlier than a lot of Vegas people.

"So, what accent am I hearin'? Minnesota?"

"Close. Wisconsin, actually." She pronounced the "o" almost like a short "a." "The accent's Great Lakes."

"Got a nice sound to it."

"So, you wan'a hit or not?"

"I'll stick."

He had a queen of diamonds and a jack of hearts. She had a deuce showing, and when she flipped over her down card, it was a ten of clubs. She hit herself with a king of spades. He'd actually been letting it ride the last four hands, so he picked up thirty-two dollars on the hand. He had a good streak going, up sixty-two bucks, and having a great time with Blake to boot.

"How about you? Where you in from?"

"I been living in Vegas since September. I'm a grad. student over at the U. Came from Long Beach."

"I didn't think you were a tourist."

"I'm staying the summer. Wan'a get a dealing job. Wha'da you think? You recommend it?"

"Sure."

"Big turnover, is there?"

"A little bit."

"How long you been doin' it?"

"A little over a year. A lota' dealers been around longer'n that, though. You got'a stick around if you wan'a go anywhere."

The irony in that statement had escaped Holdorff at the time, but he remembered it years later when he realized that he was, as he had always been and always would be, one of the vagabonds of this world constantly on the move, down the road, on to the next whatever, and wondering why.

The conversation was moving as fast as the play, and by this time, the other players had quit, replaced by three new ones. Her smiling expression hadn't changed, regardless of who was playing. The only time she looked at the players was when she asked them if they wanted a hit, and then she'd immediately turn her attention back to the cards. The pinstriped pit boss stood behind her and the other dealers, keeping an eye on all the play. The cocktail waitress in her scant outfit stopped and took Holdorff's order. A short beer.

He was struck by the contrast in appearance of the three casino employees. For although they looked so different, they all had the

The Muttering Retreats

same coolness and detached efficiency that marked their dealings with each other and the customers. Just as Holdorff was about to pick up the conversation where he left off, a relief dealer moved in and took over the table. He killed off his beer, keeping his eye on Blake. Then he picked up his chips and followed her. She was about to enter the lounge where the dealers take their breaks when he caught up with her and asked if he could buy her a cup of coffee. The impersonal, detached look that she had while dealing had almost completely vanished, and she gave him a warm smile. Holdorff thought things were looking pretty good, but then she put a damper on his hopes when she said,

"It's against house rules for employees to socialize with the customers during working hours."

"Well, then," he said. "How 'bout when you get off? Then I can even buy you a drink. Or even better yet, how would you like to go out to dinner?"

"I don't know. This is all happening pretty fast. I don't even know your name."

Holdorff told her his name; she didn't have to tell him hers. He didn't get a date that night. She already had plans for the end of her shift. He did manage to get a telephone number, which he copied on one of the poem-envelopes in the breast pocket of his corduroy sports jacket, the same corduroy sports jacket he'd bought new after he signed his first teaching contract a year and a half ago. He told her he'd be in touch. She went into the dealer's lounge as he turned and headed home, smoke trailing over his right shoulder, his pipe jutting out that corner of his mouth.

Two days later, he got a job downtown at the Pioneer Club. He called Blake to tell her the news and see if he could take her out and celebrate. They both had similar shifts with Thursdays off, so he made a lunch date for the following Thursday.

"Where in Wisconsin you from?" he asked when they met. "Not that I'd know where you're talkin' about, anyway."

"A little town called Roxbury, not far from Madison, the state capitol. Daddy's a dairy farmer near there. Big family. I'm second of five siblings. Two brothers, two sisters."

"Good university in Madison, you know."

"I know. I graduated from there two years ago," she said.

"How'd you end up dealin' cards in Vegas?

The Muttering Retreats

"Hopefully I won't be ending up here. It's a temporary stop. First place I came to where I could make any money. On my way to the west coast. Had this dream my whole life of living at the beach in California."

"You ought'a check out Belmont Shore sometime. I lived there when I was an undergraduate," Holdorff said.

"Where is it?"

"Long Beach. Not far from Los Angeles. Where I got discharged from the Navy. Went to college there. Nice place. You should check it out."

"I've already been to a couple places over there. Santa Monica and that area."

"Oh, yeah? It's pretty over there, all right, but you ought'a check out the Shore, too. 'Fact we ought'a go together sometime. I could show you around. Meet H.H."

"H.H.? Who's that?"

"My son. Go'n'a be four in August."

"So, you've been married, huh?"

"Yeah, but it didn't last long. About a year and a half. Best thing to come of it was H.H. So, how 'bout it? Wan'a go there with me sometime?"

"Well, I don't know. Don't you think we should get to know each other a little better before we plan an overnight trip?"

"Oh, absolutely. I didn't mean that we should go next week, but we could figure on sometime before summer ends."

After lunch he drove her over to campus and showed her around. She'd never been there. He took her to the studio theater where Roget was blocking the musical. They watched for a few minutes, and as they got up to leave, Roget told the cast to take five. He came over to say hello to Holdorff and to meet Blake, but he barely acknowledged Holdorff's presence, rather devoting all of his attention to the dealer.

"He was very nice to *me*," she said as they drove away from campus, "but he didn't seem too happy to see *you*. Is he mad at you?"

"'Fraid so. I wrote the lyrics to the songs in the play, and he thinks I could've done a better job on 'em."

"Huh. That's strange. What little we saw right now sounded fine to me."

"Yeah, you just got'a understand Roget. Odd duck. A real eccentric."

And that was the main reason why it didn't bother Holdorff that Roget was so attentive to her. Now, if it had been Novak back in

116

The Muttering Retreats

Long Beach, Holdorff might've been jealous, because Novak was such a hustler, but Roget was more the shiny-pants chalk pusher whose chief interest was his work in the classroom and at the studio theater.

Holdorff saw Blake regularly through the summer and into fall. In late July, the weekend before the musical opened, they both got other dealers to take their shifts and went to Long Beach. He showed her around the Shore, which she liked a lot. In fact, she liked it so much that she looked briefly at some real estate. A couple open houses. Nothing serious. She was just trying to get a feel for the market.

While they were in town, he picked H.H. up, and took him to the beach on the Alamitos Bay side of the peninsula, and lo and behold, they were right in front of Novak's apartment. He called out to them from his second-story deck and invited them up for a drink. They went up and out to the deck where they sat and chatted in the sun as Blake read to H.H. from a Dr. Seuss book. They hung around with Novak for only one drink because H.H. was getting restless and wanted to go back down to the beach. And to Holdorff's surprise and relief, Novak didn't try to make a run on Blake.

Jerome Arthur

Holdorff was amazed at how much his son had grown since he'd last seen him a year ago. Talking like crazy, and already at such a young age, talking about baseball. He told Holdorff about his best friend who lived across the park from him.

"His dad bought 'im gloves 'n' a bat 'n' ball. He's showin' us how ta play. I ain't got a glove, so I j'st use his extra one."

When he heard that, Holdorff took H.H. to Shore Sporting Goods on Second Street and bought him a Rawlings glove, "Mister Shortstop—Marty Marion." From there they went to Domenico's for pizza, and then Holdorff took the boy back to his mother. They stayed in the motel at the corner of Bayshore and Second Street across from the library. As they pulled away the next morning on their way back to the desert, Holdorff felt a pang of nostalgia for the Shore and a longing to spend more time with his son.

In Las Vegas they got back into their routines. Holdorff and Blake were together constantly, spending alternate nights in each other's apartments. They saw Roget's musical together on opening night, and they went out to dinner and the movies on their days off. When the fall semester started, Holdorff dropped the T.A.-ship

The Muttering Retreats

and went to on-call only at the Pioneer Club. It was the kind of deal that he could say yes or no when they called him to take a shift. He was cutting back on all of these extra curricular activities so that he could seriously work on his thesis.

Nine

Holdorff was dealing cards one night before the start of the fall semester, and toward the end of his shift, a man, who, he immediately guessed, was a schoolteacher or administrator, sat down at his table. He had that rumpled look that educators have, like Roget, barbered at home, short-sleeve white shirt and tie and a suit that was neat, though obviously cheap. Shiny pants chalk pusher.

"You don't look like your average black-jack dealer."

"And you're not the first one who's told me that. Wha'da you s'pose it is, the glasses?"

"That, the bushy eyebrows, the beard. You name it. You look like a student to me."

"You hit that one on the head."

"It's my job."

"Oh yeah? What job's that?"

"School district personnel director down in Needles."

The Muttering Retreats

"Yeah, well, I'm a grad. student over at the U."

There weren't any other players at the table, so it wasn't hard for Holdorff to deal and talk at the same time.

"What's your major?"

"You wan'a hit?"

"I'll stick. You didn't answer my question."

"English. Third semester M.A. candidate. Doin' my thesis on Allen Ginsberg. Dealer hits on fourteen. Seven."

Holdorff picked up the cards and put them at the bottom of the deck and the chips in the tray. The player put a couple dollar chips in the circle on the table. Then Holdorff dealt another hand.

"Ever do any teaching?" the player said as he looked at his cards.

"Wrong question. Wan'a a hit?"

"Why is that the wrong question?"

"I got a feeling if I say yes, you're go'n'a try to talk me into signing on over in Bumfuck Arizona. You wan'a hit or not?"

"Needles, California, actually. Along the shores of the beautiful Colorado River. Yeah, gi'me a hit."

"Oh, I'm impressed," Holdorff said as he hit him with a ten of clubs. The player turned over his hand. He'd hit on twelve, a king spades and a deuce of diamonds.

"It's not as bad as you're thinking."

"And if I say no, you'll go into recruiting mode. Either way, I'm stuck with you pounding my ear till I sign on the dotted line."

"'Fraid so."

"Ah' right, I plead guilty. Last year I had a job in a high school over in Long Beach. It was okay; just not my level. I wan'a get a college job. That's why I'm goin' to grad. school."

Holdorff's shift ended so he fanned the cards out on the table as a relief dealer stepped in. The player picked up his chips and caught up with him as he was heading toward the exit.

"Name's Gilmore," the player said, offering his hand. "Buy you a drink?"

Holdorff thought about it for just a moment and said, "Sure."

They went to a small lounge around the corner from the Pioneer Club. When they got settled at the bar, Holdorff ordered a Heineken. He thought, *what the hell, Gilmore's buying.*

"Okay, I'd be lying to you if I said I wasn't interested in your qualifications to teach high school English? I'm the guy who hires

122

The Muttering Retreats

teachers and staff for the whole school district, and the only position I haven't filled for the coming year is an English job in the high school. Five classes five days a week. One for each grade level, two senior classes."

"Naw, I don't think so."

"Don't give me an answer right away. Just think about it. I'm pretty desperate here. This school year got off to a bad start. I've filled every position except this one. It's a full-time teaching contract with benefits, tenure track, the whole ball a' wax."

Holdorff quickly finished his first beer, and Gilmore, who'd barely touched his, ordered him another one, picking up the tab again. They went on like that for a couple hours. Drinking three to Gilmore's one, Holdorff started to get a little tipsy.

And Gilmore carried on the whole time, telling Holdorff how much he'd like living in Needles, what a great small town atmosphere it had, friendly people, pretty women.

"If you miss all this razzle dazzle, you're only a hundred miles away down Highway Ninety-five. Only takes a couple hours to get here."

When he heard Gilmore out, and when he considered his situation at S.D.U.N. (or as

Holdorff was calling it of late, STUN), he thought taking the job in Needles might not be a bad move, but then he quickly perished the thought. The more he mulled it over, the more excuses he could think of for not taking it. He was making good money where he was, and he had steady female companionship, which he hadn't had since he was married.

He'd never been to Needles. Where the hell was it anyway? On a desert in the middle of nowhere. At least in Vegas, he had the nightlife if he wanted it. But Gilmore said it was only a couple hours away. He could come up weekends, stay with Blake. She was really all that was tying him to Las Vegas. He could see his days were numbered at S.D.U.N. His graduate committee, Roget in particular since the musical had flopped, were all over him like the cheap suit Gilmore was wearing.

The way Gilmore hustled Holdorff, he could have been a drummer from Missouri or Indiana, selling sewing machines or vacuum cleaners or bibles or encyclopedias, or, for that matter, trombones.

"So, wha'da you say. Thinking about my offer? Pays thirty-two hundred a year, plus benefits."

The Muttering Retreats

"Not enough money. I can make that much here in a month," Holdorff lied.

"There's one benefit I think you wouldn't want to pass up. Actually I'm looking for an English department chair as well as a teacher."

"Huhoho! You really are desperate. I don't have that kind of experience."

"You don't need it. I'm talking about a small district here. Just one high school. There's only one other full-time guy in the department, and a part-time gal who'd also sub. for you guys."

"How come the other guy's not department head, and why doesn't the gal take the full-time job?"

"Department chair's a rotating thing, and he did it last year. Guy who left did it year before last. The gal doesn't want full-time. She's raising a family. Married to the city manager. Also, we'd run into problems credentialing her for the administrative part of the job. Hasn't quite got her B.A. degree. Only has a provisional credential."

Holdorff nodded and thought about it.

"Department chair gets an extra five-hundred bucks a year, so you actually make thirty-seven hundred, plus the benefits."

Jerome Arthur

Holdorff had just come off a long shift at the tables, and he hadn't eaten since his break. He'd already had five beers while Gilmore was still working on his second. He was getting drunk. Puffing on his pipe and sipping on his sixth beer, he looked at Gilmore through blood-shot eyes.

"What the hell kinda' benefits you talkin' about?"

"Full hospitalization including dental and vision care. And of course you get all national holidays off including the usual two weeks at Christmas, one week at Easter and two and a half months in the summer. Hundred-eighty day schedule. It's a great job; you ought'a take it." He was working Holdorff for everything he was worth. "We've got a good little district down there in Needles, like one big happy family. You'll get along great with the rest of the faculty."

Because he was beginning to feel the effects of the beer, Holdorff didn't even notice the assurance with which Gilmore said, "you'll," not "you might," or "you would," but "you'll," as if he knew Holdorff would agree to take the job, and all he had to do now was sign the contract. Nor did he notice that Gilmore wasn't even drinking his second beer, not even

The Muttering Retreats

sipping on it a little, whereas he'd already drunk five. Emptying his sixth, Holdorff said abruptly,

"Let's get something to eat. You got time?"

"All the time in the world. You name it."

So they went to an all-night diner one block off Fremont Street, and Gilmore again picked up the tab. After they ate, they went to one of Holdorff's favorite spots, a neighborhood bar where he knew the bartender and a few of the drinking customers. They sat down at the bar and ordered two Coors on draught. When Gilmore tried to pay, Holdorff pushed his hand back and said,

"'S one's on me. Pu' cher money back in yer pocket."

Reluctantly, Gilmore did as he was told. He then watched Holdorff drink two more beers. He'd quit talking about the job for sometime now, instead listening to Holdorff's sad, drunken tale of how he was being pushed out of the M.A. program at the university. As the story unfolded, Gilmore saw his opening, saw his opportunity to snare Holdorff and make him his English teacher. He let Holdorff talk on and drink on, and when the time was right, he offered to give him a lift back to his car.

"'Kay," Holdorff slurred.

127

Jerome Arthur

They walked out of the bar, Holdorff slanting into Gilmore with his left arm draped over his shoulder, his right hand waving to the bartender. That was the last time he saw the bartender. Before Gilmore started the car, he reached into the back seat and pulled a black attaché case into the front seat. He placed it on the seat between them and took out a sheet of paper that looked like a standard contract.

"Look that over," he said, "'case you change your mind about coming to Needles. Looks like you're not going back to the university. Right?"

"Yeah. Guess not."

Holdorff looked bleary-eyed at the contract in front of him, not reading it, not even being able to read it. He began to sense the lucidity that Hemingway wrote about when a man gets drunk. Suddenly, he had a moment of clarity. The Needles job seemed to be the way to go. He saw it as a graceful exit from Las Vegas, which, he now knew, was a dead end. Needles was another place to go, an alternative.

He could see a certain advantage to teaching high school right now. At least he'd have his own classroom again, and not just be a flunky in someone else's classroom. And the more he thought about it, the better the pay sounded, too. He knew he wouldn't get rich teaching school, but the pay wasn't that bad, and the job wasn't as boring as dealing twenty-one, which he found to be extremely monotonous after only three months. Teaching teenagers how to read and write could be challenging if it was done right, and in his present clarity of mind, he started devising different ways of teaching the kinds of classes he might have. Things began to fall into place, and Holdorff could see what he was going to do and where he was going to go.

"You go' 'ny plashe I c'n shtay over 'ere, if I come righ' 'way?" he asked Gilmore. They were almost to the lot where Holdorff had parked his car.

"Sure. I've got this little cottage on my property. It's got bathroom facilities. You'll have to eat out, but you can stay there until you find a place."

Holdorff started giggling uncontrollably as he got out of Gilmore's car. He couldn't believe he was about to sign a high school contract again, but he was going to do it, and it wasn't merely a drunken whim. He was going to go through with it. He swore to himself that he would.

129

"Follow me over my plashe. Sign 'a con- trac' 'ere."

"You okay to drive?"

"Yeah. No shweat."

Gilmore followed Holdorff's shaky lead to his apartment. They went in and sat down at the kitchen table where he signed the contract. Then Holdorff went to the refrigerator and broke out two bottles of Bud from next to his bundle of songs and poems. He stood there for a few seconds with the refrigerator door open and shook his head, thinking,

...people think I'm nuts storing this stuff in here...fuck 'em...what do i care...?

Then he shook his head again, closed the door and went back over to the table and opened the two beers with the church key that was a permanent fixture along with the antique Underwood typewriter and outbox on his kitchen table.

"Here's to my new job," he said and held the bottle aloft.

Then he chugalugged it down and half slammed, half set it down on the table. Gilmore took a long pull from his, too. It was the most he'd had all night.

"Yeah. That hits the spot," he said contentedly. "Now, you're not go'n'a try to get out of it tomorrow, are you? When the glow wears off, so to speak?"

His expression changed slightly, became worried. But he was sure he had Holdorff, and Holdorff reassured him.

"Naw. Don' worry 'bout it. I'll be 'ere. Come by your plashe t'morrow af'ernoon af'er I get checked outa' here, 'n' be on the job Monday mornin'."

Gilmore put the signed contract back into the attaché case. He then wrote down his address and directions to his house and left.

Ten

Holdorff stopped by the Pioneer the next day and quit his dealing job. From there he went to the Stardust. He caught Blake as she was about to take her break. When he told her about Needles and the teaching position, she seemed glad he'd gotten the job, but disappointed that he was leaving Las Vegas. She told him she'd be down to visit him on Thursday. Since his rent was paid up to the end of the month, he gave his landlord two weeks notice and told him the place would be available as soon as he got his stuff out of there, which would be that afternoon. Then he got on the road.

Ninety-five south was deserted. The only traffic he saw was going north. He made Needles in less than two hours, and just as Gilmore had said, the little town sat alongside the Colorado River where Highways Ninety-five and Sixty-six merged. He stopped at a gas station on the outskirts of town and looked at a map

The Muttering Retreats

Scotch-taped in the window next to the service bay. Putting a match to a fresh bowl, he looked for the high school and Gilmore's street. Then he drove another half mile down Sixty-six and got off at Eagle Pass Road. The high school, a couple blocks west of there, looked old but clean, not run down in any way. The place had a positive feel to it. Since it was Saturday, the place was deserted.

He crossed back over the highway and drove to Gilmore's house, a two-storey Craftsman on Third Street, four blocks from City Hall. He pulled in the driveway. Down at the end was a one-car garage that had been converted into a studio. He guessed it was the cottage Gilmore said he could stay in until he found a place of his own.

The front porch spanned the width of the house. A glider sat to the right of the entry door. As Holdorff mounted the top step, Gilmore pushed open the screen door.

"Hey, Holdorff. How you doin'?" he said offering his hand.

"Not bad, considering how drunk I got last night. Slept in, which helped."

"Come on in. I been raking leaves. Wife's puttin' on an early dinner. Wan'a join us?"

Jerome Arthur

A pleasant aroma wafted through the dining room into the living room. They walked through to the kitchen and found Gilmore's wife cooking a stew. After Gilmore introduced them, he told Holdorff to pull his car up next to his in the back yard, and he'd meet him at the cottage. Gilmore was standing by the rear bumper of his car in the carport next to the cottage as Holdorff rolled up the drive. He directed Holdorff to a spot in a gravel area next to the carport.

Indian Summer on the desert and it was hot. Fortunately, a couple of huge sycamores that still had most of their leaves graced Gilmore's large lot, providing shade for Holdorff's car and new home. Gilmore told Holdorff that he'd converted the garage into an art studio for his wife. She'd moved her things into the house in anticipation of his arrival. After he got his suitcase unloaded, he and Gilmore went back into the house where Gilmore's wife was just putting dinner on the table. Their kids were grown and out of the house, so it was just the three of them.

His first week of teaching was uneventful. Needles kids were generally good kids. Small-town kids. Blake got into town at four on Thursday, and they spent the rest of the afternoon entwined in love. They went to dinner at a

The Muttering Retreats

Mexican restaurant on Front Street, and did more of the same all night long back at Holdorff's place. This raised eyebrows in the Gilmore household and neighborhood. She was on her way back to Las Vegas when he started his first class at nine on Friday morning.

After that visit he knew he had to find a place of his own. He picked up a *Desert Star* on Saturday morning and found a trailer for rent in a court near the river. He was out of Gilmore's cottage by Saturday afternoon.

Over all Holdorff's stay in Needles wasn't a pleasant one. The small-town atmosphere that Gilmore had touted so eagerly was too confining for him. He was going stir after the first month. He felt like he was losing his anonymity. Everybody knew everybody else's business. He got disapproving looks from people on a Saturday afternoon when he stepped out onto the sidewalk in front of his favorite downtown bar. That was hardly appropriate behavior for the high school English teacher. He discouraged Blake from visiting him again, and that put a strain on their relationship because she liked the small-town atmosphere of Needles. It reminded her of home, and she saw it as a perfect escape from Las Vegas. But he didn't want her coming to visit him again, so he'd go to her, and he'd go every weekend. The best part of the deal was his job. He got along great with the kids. It's all that sustained him until the weekend, and the combination of the students and the weekends was all that kept him going till the end of the school year.

So, he kept at it for the nine months of his contract, and in June, he headed back to Long Beach. Blake left Las Vegas and went with him. They found a one-bedroom apartment on Ocean Boulevard in the Shore. Holdorff got his job back in the produce section of the A & P. Blake got a job as a checker, but immediately put in an application for a teaching job in the Long Beach school district. As they lived under the same roof and worked in the same store through the summer, they suffered from too much togetherness. It didn't take long for them to get on each other's nerves.

Just when they thought they were about to kill each other, she got hired for a fifth grade job at Horace Mann Elementary School. She began her contract in September and started taking night classes at Long Beach State. If she wanted to continue teaching, she would eventually have to get an elementary teaching credential. She also started to look for a house to buy, and by Halloween, she had a two-bedroom bun-

The Muttering Retreats

galow on Nieto Avenue in escrow. She moved into her house the weekend before Thanksgiving, and Holdorff stayed behind in the apartment. They remained friends and lovers. They just couldn't live together.

Holdorff started the M.A. program at State in the fall. He also landed a teaching assistantship, so he once again gave up his job pushing produce. At the time a T.A. at Long Beach State was nothing more than a lackey to the three professors who ran the remedial English clinic. The T.A.'s only duty was to read essays written by students who had scored low on the college entrance exam. After they read the papers, they went over them with the students individually, tutoring them on the finer points of grammar and composition. The prof's. were the only ones doing any teaching. They conducted one-hour lectures on Tuesdays and Thursdays.

Holdorff and the other teaching assistants were treated like a staff of servants. His year-and-a-half teaching experience meant nothing to the trio of prof's. he graded papers for. They reminded the clinicians constantly that they were "apprentice teachers." The last time he'd endured that kind of berating was when he was in Navy boot camp.

Jerome Arthur

Holdorff wasn't your average teaching assistant. The younger clinicians, who were all a good five years his junior, were, to Holdorff's way of thinking, idealistic and naïve. Holdorff, on the other hand, had grown cynical over the years. He saw far too much irony in life to be as idealistic as they were. There were a couple of other guys around Holdorff's age, but they had their cynicism more under control than he did. One was a couple years older. They were all Korean War veterans. None of the other clinicians were veterans of any kind, and the difference between the two was like night and day.

Holdorff wasn't working in the clinic for the money. It wasn't that good. And he wasn't in it for the abuse, either. The main reason he stuck it out was because he saw it as an opportunity to be a mentor to the younger clinicians. As a high school English teacher, he was really only a disciplinarian to his students and a colleague to the other teachers. As clinicians, he and his veteran buddies were teachers to the students, and mentors to the younger clinicians. Their youthful idealism reminded him of himself when he was that age. He remembered when he used to find all kinds of meanings in subjects as diverse as Renaissance English po-

The Muttering Retreats

etry and twentieth century absurdist drama. Now he was watching them do the same thing.

"Why do you read those writers?" Holdorff would ask, with as much sarcasm as he could muster. "All Faulkner and Hemingway ever did was make life miserable for grad. students. If they hadn't written all that stuff, you all wouldn't have to read it."

Smoke snorted out his nostrils as he dragged in two or three more puffs, holding a match between thumb and forefinger over the bowl cupped in his right hand.

Besides his veteran brothers, there was one other clinician his age. Her name was Steinberg, and Holdorff thought of her as being just as much man as woman. She was an officious shrew, dressing daily in a dark business suit (her maleness). Her sharp features prompted the other clinicians to call her "hatchet face" behind her back. The harshness of her shrill voice highlighted her femaleness, but it was hardly feminine.

Everywhere he'd gone in life, from grammar school on through college, he'd had to deal with someone calling him "Holdoff," and in the clinic that person was Steinberg. Whenever it happened, the person would pronounce it right, once corrected. Roget did it. Not Stein-

berg. She seemed to mispronounce it intention-
ally, knowing it irritated him. It was the Navy
all over again, being cast with people you can't
escape. Or like the family scene, which he
didn't have first hand knowledge of, but he'd
heard from plenty of other people how it was,
being stuck with people because you're related
to them, not because you like them and want to
be with them, people you'd never choose as
friends.

The T.A.-ship entitled him to a study
cubicle in the library, and that compensated
somewhat for the bad vibes emanating from Steinberg and the rest of the clinic scene, but what
really mitigated any bad feelings was the handicapped parking sticker he managed to get. A
real bonanza. He got his cane out of the closet
and took his medical discharge with him to register for classes. When he got to the table where
they were selling parking stickers, he hobbled
up and showed the guy issuing them his medical
discharge, and without really looking at it, he
gave Holdorff the handicapped sticker.

"I believe in living comfortably," he
later told the other clinicians.

The study cubicle was also for sheer
convenience and comfort. He was glad he got it,
even though he didn't spend a lot of time there.

The Muttering Retreats

In fact, it seemed he loaned it out more than he used it himself. He really didn't spend much time around the library at all. If he didn't have a class, he didn't go to campus. He did all his writing in the apartment on Ocean Boulevard, and he spent all the rest of his spare time with H.H. and Blake. He also hooked up with Novak at least once a week for a Heineken at Hoefly's.

Eleven

Holdorff's first call after he got back in town was to H.H. He hadn't seen the boy since last summer when he and Blake had visited. Seeing him again gave Holdorff a positive feeling at a time when he needed all the positive feelings he could get. While the rest of the world appeared to be moving ahead without him, Holdorff found comfort and security in the fact that at least he had a bloodline to the future.

If he loved anyone, he loved his son. He'd only professed love to one woman, the one he'd married. He barely remembered anything about his mother, so he didn't know if he loved her or not. He was pretty sure he didn't love his father. He knew positively that he didn't like him very much. He was pretty sure he loved Blake. H.H. was the only one left. And now the boy was getting to an age that Holdorff could relate to him more as a person than as a baby. He'd been born with his mother's Polynesian

The Muttering Retreats

features and Holdorff's Scandinavian coloring including a hint of reddish-blond in his dark hair. As he matured, he was becoming a very good-looking little boy, and Holdorff could see that he would be a handsome young man when he reached adolescence and adulthood.

His best buddy at that young age was the son of a friend of Holdorff's ex-wife from City College. The friend had married a catcher from City's baseball team. That father was already teaching his son, Johnny, the fundamentals of the game. He'd bought the boy a couple of baseball gloves, a ball and a bat when he was only two years old. They lived on the other side of the park from Holdorff's ex-wife and son, and Johnny's father got them together in the park a couple times a week and tried to teach them to throw, hit and catch the ball. Now that H.H. had his own glove, he didn't have to borrow Johnny's extra one. The father used it when he played catch with the two boys. They were only five years old, so they weren't physically developed enough to be any good, but they were catching on, and Holdorff's son was developing a keen interest in the game.

That interest went beyond just learning how to play. Johnny's dad was an avid Angels fan, and he'd taken the boys to Wrigley Field a

143

couple times that spring to see them play. After the second time he'd gone, H.H. really started to follow the game. He'd gotten a program and learned the names of the players in the Angels' starting line-up. He looked at the baseball pictures in the sports section of the *Press-Telegram* as his mother read the captions out loud, and he'd started a good collection of Topps bubble gum trading cards. He had Mickey Mantle, Bob Gibson, Bill Mazeroski, Moose Skowron, Ernie Banks, Orlando Cepeda, and Warren Spahn, all the big names of the day, plus others.

H.H. watched the game of the week on Saturdays with Johnny and his dad. Sometimes Holdorff would join them when he picked the boy up for his weekend visit. They'd watch the game with the other boy and his dad and then take off from there. Holdorff had come a long way since the first time he tried to pick H.H. up. Now he was spending the whole weekend with him, no problem.

Holdorff got his fill of baseball in one sitting with those three guys, but that was all right. The good time he was having hanging with H.H. far outweighed the boredom of watching baseball games on television, and it brought back good memories of Roget who knew so much about old time baseball lore.

The Muttering Retreats

He'd known batting averages of the greatest players and scores of historic games. He'd known nicknames such as Shoeless Joe Jackson, the Flying Dutchman, the Yankee Clipper, and of course the Bambino. Holdorff didn't know any of these things. The names and scores and averages only swirled around in his head.

H.H. was developing that same kind of interest in the contemporary game. He and Johnny would put their mitts on and slug the pocket as they watched a game on television. H.H. took his cue from Johnny and his dad and was an Angels fan. It was their first year in the American League. His favorite player on the team was their first baseman, Steve Bilko. He liked Bilko best because he hit a lot of home runs. His favorite pitcher was Bob Gibson of the Saint Louis Cardinals. One Saturday morning when Holdorff went to pick H.H. up, he was at Johnny's house watching a game, so he trekked across the park and knocked on the door.

"I'd kinda' like to take the boys to the Angels game today," Johnny's dad said when he answered his knock. "Wan'a go? They're playin' the Yankees."

"Ah, could we, Pop?" H.H. chimed in.

"Yeah, that sounds like a swell idea,"

Holdorff said, not really caring what teams were playing. He didn't know one from another.

"Yanks'll prob'ly slaughter 'em," said Johnny's dad. "Angels're an expansion team this year, so they ain't no good. They're in the cellar so far, along with the Kansas City A's."

"Hey, you couldn't prove it by me. Let's go. Should be fun."

"We'll prob'ly see a lota' home runs. Bilko'll be good for one or two, and Maris and Mantle're competing to break Babe Ruth's single season record. Wrigley's a perfect home run park. Power alleys're the shortest in the league."

Holdorff didn't have the foggiest idea what he was talking about, but he knew he'd have a good time. It was a beautiful day, and this was the perfect opportunity for him to spend sometime with H.H. on H.H.'s own turf. It also saved him from having to figure out where to take H.H. and what to do with him. He knew he could never show him as good a time as they'd have at the ballpark. For Holdorff it was a new experience, and he looked at it as educational. And he would soon learn that going to a game at the ballpark was so much better than watching it on television.

And so the four of them went to the game and had a great time. They got seats in the

The Muttering Retreats

right field bleachers. The two boys took their gloves, hoping to catch a home run. They didn't quite *catch* one, but Maris did hit one that bounced off one of the benches and landed about ten feet away from Johnny's dad. He beat a couple other guys to it and picked it up.

"Okay, boys," he said. "Now we can use this one to practice with."

As the afternoon wore on, the two men bought their boys Angels baseball caps and pennants. They had a couple beers and the boys had Cokes. When the game ended, they drove back to Long Beach, and Holdorff took H.H. to his apartment in the Shore. As H.H. napped, Holdorff sat down to work on a song.

Just had to go Away

The last time I saw you,
I finally realized
That my presence only
Annoyed you as much as your
Absence saddened me.

(Refrain)
I'll say it again—
I just wanted to be your friend,
But you told me not to stay
So I just had to go away.

Jerome Arthur

It was near the end I saw
A look in your eyes that
Told me I should leave you alone
And not come back again,
But that was too hard.
(Refrain)

I tried to talk you out of
What you'd talked yourself into,
But I could see you had your
Mind made up to do what
You'd already decided.
(Refrain)

So I'll just deny myself,
As hard as it is to do.
I'll force myself to stay
Away from you since it
Seems it's what you want.
(Refrain)

Blake showed up as he was transcribing it from the cancelled envelope.

"You have a good time?" she asked after Holdorff told her what they'd done that day.

"Great time. Wore H.H. out. He's takin' a nap."

"Wan'a go for pizza when he wakes up?"

"Good idea. Take him back to his mother after that."

148

The Muttering Retreats

They left Domenico's at around seven o'clock and got H.H. home by seven-thirty. Then they went back to her house and watched *Rawhide* on T.V. before going to bed.

Twelve

Holdorff got enrolled in the M.A. program at State in the fall. Blake was teaching fifth grade and taking classes on Tuesday and Thursday nights. They remained good friends after her move and still spent a couple evenings a week together. Holdorff went to the Forty Niners on the nights he didn't get together with Blake.

Invariably, he'd check out happy hour at the Forty Niners on Friday afternoons. That was when and where he met another teacher from State named McSwayne. Holdorff had heard of McSwayne around the department, had seen his name in the schedule of classes, but he'd never met him or taken a class from him, so he wasn't even sure what he looked like. That's why when he sat next to him at the bar, he only vaguely recognized him.

"Been a hell of a week," said Holdorff, sipping his beer. "Had two papers due, one on

The Muttering Retreats

Wednesday, one today. Barely got 'em both done on time."

"Student at State?" McSwayne asked.

"Yeah, you?"

"Prof."

"Oh yeah? What department?"

"English. Comp. lit."

"You know, I thought I recognized you from somewhere. I'm in English, too. Grad. student, American lit. Probably seen you around the department."

They shook hands and introduced themselves.

"You looked familiar to me, too," McSwayne said.

"Don't think I've seen you in here before."

"'Cause it's the first time I've been here. First joint I saw after I left campus. Needed a quick beer. I had a rough week, too. Especially today."

"Really? What happened?"

"Second time I got passed over for tenure."

"That's tough."

"Yeah, it is."

"Hope you make it next time."

"Oh, I'll get it. Question is, when?"

"God, I guess. I'm reading papers in the remedial English clinic, and all three of the prof's. in charge down there've got tenure, and they're all pretty bad. Must be politics. Although, sometimes they get it right. I got another buddy in the department got tenure, Novak, and he's good. Know 'im?"

"He's a buddy of mine, and you're right. He's good. You hit the nail on the head when you said politics. It's all politics. They're always trying to give Novak a ration of shit, but they can't touch him 'cause he's got tenure."

They chatted for a few more minutes as McSwayne finished his beer. Holdorff had two more beers after McSwayne left, and then he headed home. He took a walk on the beach and watched the sunset over Palos Verdes peninsula. Then he went back to his apartment and wrote a song. Earlier in the week, he'd gone downtown Long Beach to look for something to write about, and he found himself at a city council meeting. After hearing McSwayne's story about his tenure, he thought again about that city council meeting, and it gave him the idea for the song.

The Muttering Retreats

City Hall Blues

Took a walk on down to City Hall.
Thought I'd see how the government faired.
There was a hearing a-going on to stall
The opening of a shop for hair.
The applicant had received the call
To stop a-cuttin' on his barber chair.

(Refrain)
What a deal to pay the price,
And not have to do it twice.

The fools got up to speak their piece,
All a-talkin' an' not sayin' much.
The debate went on; it wouldn't cease.
The more talk, the more outa' touch;
Just when the rhetoric would decrease,
They started talkin' 'bout traffic 'n' such.
(Refrain)

The affordable housing contingent
Took the stand to make their appeal
To get on with building a tenement.
One guy got up acting like a big wheel
And said he couldn't afford the rent,
But soon a councilman said he'd make a deal.
(Refrain)

When they all finally wound down,
One fool nodded, fell asleep at the podium.
When he saw this, the chairman frowned,

153

And looked at the cat with odium,
But it didn't really turn things 'round.
They all danced to a nickelodeon.
(Refrain)

Now all they needed were some jugglers
To liven up a bit of the action,
But all they had were vocal strugglers
Who couldn't get their satisfaction.
It's said there were some smugglers
Making off with the liberal faction.
(Refrain)

Decided to walk on out the door
And find my way back to my pad,
But that freak crowd stayed in my head to roar,
And it was all so very sad
To see them do another encore.
When they're outa' my head, I'll be glad.
(Refrain)

He finished the song, disposed of the original and the carbon, each in its respective receptacle, and called Blake. She invited him over, and he spent the night with her.

On Monday Holdorff looked up McSwayne in his office in the English department. He was sitting at his desk looking at a brochure of Maui.

"What's happening?" said Holdorff.

The Muttering Retreats

"Hey, what're you up to?" McSwayne said, looking up from his brochure. He stood up and offered his hand across the desk.

"'Bout five-seven, but I don't think I'll get any taller."

"Very funny."

"What're *you* up to?"

"Oh, just looking over this brochure I picked up last month when the wife and I were in Lahaina."

"Maui?"

"Yup. Thinking about buying a place over there. Good investment right now."

"Hey, why not? If you can afford it."

"Yeah…well, we don't have kids, and I don't think we're go'n'a have any, so yes, we can afford it."

"I hear Hawaii's beautiful. Never been there, but my ex-wife's mother was born and raised there, and the way she talks about it, sounds like a real paradise."

"Yes it is. First time there we fell in love with the place, and we keep going back."

"You got time to go get something to eat?"

"Hey, that sounds good. Where?"

"We could walk over to the Forty Niner, get a beer and a Special."

"Let's go."

As they ate their sandwiches, Holdorff told McSwayne about the clinic follies, and McSwayne just laughed. He knew the three prof's. who ran the place, and he was well aware of their quirks. He'd witnessed those quirks many times at faculty senate meetings. He said he and Novak would sit there and laugh at those guys. After Holdorff had finished eating, he lit his pipe and continued telling McSwayne, spraying tobacco around as he gesticulated with a burnt match over the bowl.

"Should've seen Dillman the other day. Know him?"

"Not really. Seems like a strange little fellow."

"God, *I guess*. You know, his mother drops him off on campus every morning? Pulls up in a newer Buick Century, and he gets out with his briefcase and his lunch in a brown paper sack. You'd think he was still in grade school."

"Yeah, I've seen 'im. How's he do in front of a class of remedial English students."

"*So* boring. The other day he was trying to get the class to distinguish between 'siege' and 'cease,' but he wasn't telling them how he wanted them to make the distinction, whether by sound or definition, or what. They were just confused by the question."

He imitated the dapper little Dillman trying to wipe chalk dust from his suit coat lapel with his sleeve, which he held between four fingers and the heel of his hand.

"Some of the students looked at each other and snickered when he transferred the chalk dust from his lapel to his sleeve."

"He is, indeed, a funny little man. About like most of the people I work with but not Novak. He's not like that at all."

"Oh, yeah, I know. Novak's cool."

"You know, it might not be such a bad thing that I got passed over again. I've had it, if you know what I mean. I'm go'n'a start looking for a junior college job. My wife teaches biology at City, and it seems like she's got it a lot easier. Teaching load's a little heavier, but there's no pressure at all to get published."

"Hey, some of the best classes I ever had were at City."

"Yeah, well, I'm not sure I want to work at the same school with my wife, so I think I'll apply out in Orange County. Fullerton, Orange Coast, places like that. I'll try City, too, but only as a second or third choice. I *will* have to keep working, though. At least for a little while longer. I've got too many things I wan'a do that cost money. But eventually I'm looking to get out all together. I've had it with education. Been doing it fifteen years, counting my undergraduate studies. I'm bored."

"Hell, I'm bored, and I've only been at it half that long."

"Real estate'll be my ticket out. I've already bought some property. I got a cabin on an acre in Big Bear and some acreage up north in Grass Valley. My house is mortgaged to the hilt. Now I'm looking for something in Maui. I'd kind of like to get a house I could use at Christmas and Easter and rent out the rest of the year. Maybe retire there."

"How come you don't wan'a use it for the summer when you got three months off."

"Too hot in Hawaii in the summer. That's why Christmas and Easter are perfect."

"Sounds like a plan."

"Hey, it's a good way to go. You ought'a think about investing in real estate yourself, and there's no time like the present. It's cheap right now, but it'll do nothing but go up. Mark my words."

They finished their beers, walked back to campus, and went to their respective classes.

The Muttering Retreats

Over the next nine months, Holdorff and McSwayne got together every couple weeks or so for a beer at the Forty Niners. Each time they met, Holdorff noticed their differences. McSwayne drove Holdorff crazy with his patter, indeed his preaching, about the values of real estate ownership, and he whined and bitched and pissed and moaned about how much money it was costing him for trips to far away places like Hawaii. The irony was not lost on Holdorff that as he was trying to break into academia, McSwayne was trying to break out.

"It all depends on where you're coming from," McSwayne said. "I've been in college so long it feels like prison, and now I wan'a crash out like Bogey's 'Mad Dog' Roy Earle. I need time off for good behavior."

"Yeah, but a land baron?"

"Hey, why not?"

Indeed, why not? So he watched McSwayne travel about, and listened to his belly-aching about the cost. And the more he heard, the more he realized there was something to be said for the tax benefits and the profits to be made in real estate investment. However, there was a patronizing tone in the way McSwayne explained it that irritated Holdorff, and this, more than anything, turned Holdorff off to the

159

message. McSwayne took on a more-knowledgeable-than-thou attitude, and that, to Holdorff, seemed typical of many of the college professors he'd come in contact with over the years. McSwayne had more in common with Dillman than he'd ever own up to.

Many times he gave Holdorff a look that said, "Why don't you wise up. You're going nowhere and you'll never amount to anything if you keep doing it the way you're doing," but it was only a look, never a declaration. For all his preaching, McSwayne knew that Holdorff would never develop an interest in real estate. His interest would always be in the arts: literature, music, theater, film, bohemian interests, as far as McSwayne was concerned.

Holdorff especially didn't like the ancillary "benefits" that came with McSwayne's real estate boom, like shopping centers, which he tried to avoid whenever he could. McSwayne thought of them as conveniences and had no problem patronizing them. Holdorff thought of them as metastasizing tumors. They were slick and glossy, texture less, and the people who made use of them seemed insensitive and unaware of the shades and nuances of the real world. But then, what was the real world? One man's reality is another man's fantasy.

The Muttering Retreats

Holdorff likened the shopping centers to the casinos on Fremont Street and the Strip. He'd seen all the same kinds of people at both, plain-looking middle Americans whose mediocrity was palpable. Centers in Downey and Lakewood, and the newer ones out in Orange County, were identical as far as he was concerned. You had to stop and think for a minute to remember where you were. One saving grace was prices were usually pretty good, so Holdorff found himself shopping there now and again. He bought his corduroy sports jacket with the leather patches on the elbows at Cal Stores.

McSwayne was of a different point of view. On the one hand, he liked shopping malls, tract houses and freeways, yet on the other hand, he seemed to be doing everything in his power to escape them by buying property in remote places. It was mind boggling to Holdorff how a supposedly sensitive person, who'd studied authors from Homer to Dante to Goethe to Gräss and who was well-versed in them as Holdorff knew McSwayne to be, could be so crass as to advocate cheap development for the sake of making a quick buck. And that was why Holdorff didn't get as close to McSwayne as he'd gotten to Tavisón, Novak and Roget. In fact, they only remained friendly until the end of the

161

Jerome Arthur
the school year when Holdorff got accepted in
the Ph.D. program at U.S.C.

Thirteen

Holdorff's first day in the remedial English clinic got him thinking about skipping out of grad. school at State. He got his application off to Southern Cal. He'd also applied at Chapman College out in Orange County because he'd overheard a couple of the clinicians talking about how easy it was to get into the program and to get a Ph.D. from there. He didn't really want to go there, but he would have if he hadn't gotten into S.C. The third school he'd sent an application to was U.C.L.A., but he didn't get accepted there.

When he finally did get accepted at S.C., he got a bad case of buyer's remorse. He began to question his own motives. It all seemed so clear and simple when he started out with Rheinhardt and Tavisón. Back then it was all about learning. Now it had become a quest for a lousy piece of paper. And to what end? He damn sure didn't want to end up spending the rest of his life hanging around with the likes of McSwayne, Dillman and all those who'd given Roget such a bad time. And if he could only find the key to getting his song lyrics out there.

If he could do that, he could say to hell with getting that piece of paper, and to hell with hanging around with a bunch of academics and start hanging around with songwriters.

Even pushing produce sometimes appealed to him more than the academic life. He liked the people he worked with at the A & P more than those he knew on campus. They seemed more genuine and down-to-earth than the campus crowd. He was beginning to see academia as an elitist cult rooted in the juvenile politics of high school, where all the participants are in a popularity contest. The difference in the clientele was stark. Unlike the students, who were the bright-eyed, eager-to-learn clientele of the ivory tower, the customers at the produce counter were more akin to its tenured professors and administrators, arrogant, self-indulgent, not caring much about the feelings of others. He certainly thought the old adage about working with the public was true: "when you're dealing with assholes, you're go'n'a have to put up with a certain amount of shit."

The Muttering Retreats

During this period, the clientele became the fodder for his poetry, and when he'd review a finished poem, he was painfully aware of his emerging negative attitude:

My Pen Weeps

My pen weeps;
My words seep.
My heart rains
'Cause of the pains
Of living.
No one's giving,
Only taking
Till we're aching
Because their
Devil-may-care
Selfishness
Is passionless.
I'll go on,
Fly like a swan
Till I get free
Of this misery.
I won't let them
Poison my pen.

He found it interesting that a poem would start out negative and end on a positive note, and then in the next poem or song, the negativity would be tempered by nostalgia. He spent a lot of his time reminiscing. He'd get sudden urges to go back to places where he'd lived when he was growing up. He'd hear songs on the radio that brought back memories of his high school or Navy days, and he'd sing along with them. He'd hear Nat King Cole doing "Mona Lisa," and he'd have fond memories of Rheinhardt. He also absolutely could not let his negative attitude intrude on his relationship with H.H., and in fact any time he wrote anything about the boy, it bordered on the sentimental.

Eleven

The experts say no,
You can't hit 'em, but
I say what do they know?
They're just in a rut.

You got no reason,
Or so they tell me.
Almost like treason,
If you don't agree.

Take a two-year-old
And try to discuss
If he should be told
Without makin' a fuss.

The years will pass by;
'Fore you know he'll be nine,
And you'll be asking why

The Muttering Retreats
Does he still whine?

The best is yet to come.
You just wait for them
To chew bubblegum
And start to condemn.

So you just hold on
Wishing he were two
Again, but that's gone,
And really so are you.

No, he'll never see
Two again, but will
See twenty-three;
It gives me a chill.

He finished up the year at State, but didn't complete the course work, and didn't get an M.A. degree. He went away to U.S.C., and after over four years in that program, was still a long way from completing the course work he should have finished in just three years. He hadn't even started his dissertation in that time. He was lucky they let him take the comprehensives at all. This had to be the deepest, darkest hole he'd ever been in, and it was reflected in his verse:

My Thought Dreams

No one was saved,
Though the road was paved
To a bright tomorrow
With not a hint of sorrow
To be found in the slipstreams
Of my thought dreams.

All the people were betrayed
As they got ready to fade
When they all did realize
They awaited their own demise.
All the same themes
In my thought dreams.

There was darkness all 'round
And nary a sound
Could be heard from within
When the end was to begin,
And shone no bright gleams
From my thought dreams.

Now all's been paid back,
No blood left on the track.
They were all God-fearing,
But no one was hearing
Any of the screams
Of my thought dreams.

One bright spot during this time was that
he, H.H., and Blake remained close. He'd spend
a couple weekends a month with her in Belmont

The Muttering Retreats

Shore, and he'd pick up H.H. and hang out with him as well. It took Blake two years to finish her course work for her teaching credential. She only had one more year to get tenure in the Long Beach district.

He didn't make his first trip back to the A & P until his second semester at S.C. It was a busy Saturday, so his stop there was a brief one. He talked with the ladies at the check stands and bagged groceries for them. He went behind the meat counter and talked to the butcher, and he helped out the guy who'd replaced him at the produce counter. It was a good visit, once again reminding him how much more he liked the working life than the academic life.

He walked up the street to the Acapulco Inn, the same bar he'd gone into a few years before when he'd seen the two young sailors telling their friends about their adventure to Australia. He sat next to the fireplace and sipped his beer. The ping-pong table was still in the back room, but nobody was playing. There was a baseball game on the television near the front door. Three guys sat at the bar watching it, and since the bar wasn't busy, the bartender was up there with them.

Holdorff drank down his beer and walked up the street to the Beachcomber. He ordered a beer at the bar and went outside to the patio where one of his veteran buddies from the clinic was sitting in the sun watching a couple guys playing ping-pong. As Holdorff approached him, he said,

"Hey, Werdmüller. How's it goin'?"

"Hey, Holdorff. 'S goin' good. Hows 'bout yourself?"

"Not bad. You finally get your M.A.?"

"Took me three semesters, but I got it. Last January. You still up at S.C.?

"Yup."

"Got much longer to go?"

"'Nother couple years? You get a job?"

"Not full-time, but I got a couple remedial English classes at Compton two nights a week. Puttin' in my last semester in the clinic. Extra money comes in handy, but it's a demeaning job."

"Yeah, it is. How can you do it?"

"It ain't easy. Can you believe it? Steinberg got a tenure track job."

"You shittin' me? Where?"

"Long Beach City."

"Oh, wow! Wonder how Tavisón's dealing with *her*. Probably just ignores her."

"Who's Tavisón?"

"Teacher I had at City. Cool guy."

170

The Muttering Retreats

Holdorff talked with Werdmüller for about an hour, and then Werdmüller took off, leaving him to finish his last beer alone. He decided to go up to the Forty Niners. That was about as close to campus as he cared to go. He figured he'd probably run into somebody from State at the bar. As he approached the signal at Pacific Coast Highway to make his left turn from Second, he saw Tavisón making a left off P.C.H. onto Westminster Boulevard, so instead of getting into the left turn lane, Holdorff went straight when the signal changed, and he raced to catch up with him. When he finally flagged him down, he told Tavisón to meet him at the Forty Niners.

"So, how goes it?" Tavisón asked as they sipped their beers. "What're you up to these days?"

"Been going to grad. school at U.S.C.," Holdorff mumbled, lighting his pipe.

"Really? Last time I saw you, you were on your way to Las Vegas."

"Been that long? Didn't even last three full semesters there. Already been back here a couple years."

"No kiddin'."

"Yeah. Spent a year at State. Didn't finish, but I did get into S.C., so I moved up there."

171

"Thought about what you're go'n'a do your dissertation on?"

"Not really. Probably Eliot. Say, I hear Steinberg's working out at City."

"Yeah. Just started in January. You know her?"

"Worked with her in the remedial English clinic up at State. A real piece of work."

"You can say that again. Haven't known her long enough to judge, but she seems like a real ball breaker."

"How'd she get the job?"

"Don't know. I wasn't on the interview committee. Some strange people getting into education these days. And so many more want in. Future's not looking good from where I sit. I don't even know how solid *my* future is."

"You won't ever get outa' teaching," Holdorff said.

He wasn't implying that Tavisón was in a rut, or that he was stuck in a dead end job for the rest of his life. Rather, he was complimenting him. He thought Tavisón was in the best possible place, a good teacher who ought to stay in the classroom.

"I don't know," said Tavisón. He had a distant look in his eye. "Sometimes I think I might be better off doin' something else."

The Muttering Retreats

"Perish the thought. You ought'a stay right where you are."

"I guess."

"And the clientele needs you now more than ever. The first wave of baby boomers is just coming on the college scene. The first group to be raised on television. I think you're go'n'a see a lot more of 'em not knowing how to read and write. And it won't be because they can't do it. Too much hassle. You can already see it happening."

"Yeah, I know. I'm seeing it in the themes their handing in. They're *so* undisciplined. We'll just have to see how it all works out. Speaking of writing, how's yours comin' along? You still at it?"

"Oh yeah. I have my ups and downs, but I try to write at least one poem or song every day. Seems like when times are tough, I do my best work. Goin' through my divorce, I was on fire. Seems like the last couple years the flame's been dampered. I'm just go'n'a keep at it. Every couple weeks, I send in a stack of ten songs to various agents up in Los Angeles. Most of the time, they just come back unopened. Sometimes they don't come back. I don't know if they're trashing 'em or if they're holding onto them to use later. I don't ever hear anything I've written on the radio, but I don't hear everything."

"That's good. At least you're sending stuff in."

"I've sent off three bound volumes of poems I've written over the last ten years. Sent 'em to a lot of agents and publishers. I'm spending more money on postage than I'm making off of it. And I'm getting tired of the college scene. Turning into a campus bum. Startin' to feel like Bill Bishop."

Bill Bishop was the mythical (as far as Holdorff was concerned) City College student who'd started one semester ahead of Holdorff and was still taking classes there ten years later. Holdorff had never had a class with him and had never seen him in the two years he was at City, so he wasn't even sure the guy existed.

"It's all true," Holdorff said. "I really do get a sense of achievement from the writing itself, but when I finish a poem or song, I can't get the damn thing published, and it's frustrating as hell. So, I'll just keep writing it down and sending it in; if something happens, that'll be fine. If nothing happens, that'll be okay, too."

Tavisón watched as Holdorff sucked on his pipe, blowing smoke out his nostrils and inhaling right behind it. Between drags he gesticu-

The Muttering Retreats

lated, broadcasting tobacco and dying embers randomly across the resined wood bar. Tavisón envied his independence, and he remembered how insecure Holdorff had been when he was taking his remedial English class. Back then he knew that Holdorff had the intelligence and the confidence to do anything he wanted, but Tavisón also knew that Holdorff needed someone to tell him how smart he was. He was certainly smarter than he thought he was. Suddenly, Tavisón felt a twinge of pride because he had been one of the first people to tell him that.

"How's H.H. doing?" Tavisón asked.

"Fine. Growing like a weed. He's nine years old, crazy about baseball. I'm go'n'a call him in a little while and go pick him up. Maybe take him out and buy him a sundae."

"How about your ex-wife? She ever get married again?"

"Nope. She and H.H. are still living at her mother's place. I'm going out with a gal I met in Las Vegas. She moved back here with me, but now she has her own place. She got her credential from State. Got a fifth grade job at Horace Mann."

"You go'n'a get married again?"

"Nah. We tried living together. Didn't work out."

They sipped their beers, not talking for a while.

"I got'a hit the road," Tavisón said, drinking the last of his beer. "Wife and I are going out tonight, and I got'a start gettin' ready."

"Hey, yeah. Great to see yuh again! Glad I ran into you."

"Good to see you, too. Don't be strangers, and keep me posted on your progress in school. If you ever get your Ph.D. or even your masters, apply at City. For whatever it's worth, I'll give you a recommendation. And whatever you do, keep on writing and sending it in."

Tavisón got off his barstool and headed out the swinging doors of the Forty Niners. This was the second time that day that a friend had left Holdorff to finish his beer alone. It would be the last time they'd see each other for quite a long time. A couple years down the road Holdorff would be in trouble at U.S.C., and when things fell apart there, he'd move to Santa Cruz and try to get into the Ph.D. program there.

Fourteen

Holdorff couldn't remember exactly when his antipathy for television began. It had to have been during his marriage. His ex-wife was a T.V. junkie. He remembered her watching situation comedies like "I Love Lucy" and "The Honeymooners." The laugh track was the only laughter in the room. He didn't get it. He thought the commercials were phony. They featured an actor in a white coat saying stuff like, "More doctors smoke mentholated Kools than any other brand." That slogan later morphed into "I'd rather fight than switch," featuring an actor with a shoe-polish-smudged black eye and smoking a Tareyton. And the empty programming continued with *Sugarfoot* and *Cheyenne* in the 'fifties, and *The Wild Wild West* and *The Rifleman* in the 'sixties.

Holdorff didn't own a T.V. set. The only time he watched was when he was with Blake, and then he'd get up and go out on the front porch and take a couple puffs from his pipe during the commercials. Thus, he'd only seen bits and pieces of shows and commercials. He wondered what the attraction was. Sometimes he thought the show at the neighborhood laundromat in front of the round glass window of one of the dryers could be just as entertaining.

His aversion really got intense when his wife made him get a television set after they were married. She had insisted on it. Her mother was the first in their neighborhood to get a T.V., so she'd already been watching for a year or two when he met her. When they first started going out together, he was so blinded by love that he didn't notice just how much time she spent in front of the T.V. set, and after they got married, that time increased to the point that she was staying up all night watching old movies and smoking cigarettes. She seemed hypnotized by the prime-time stuff. It was during this time that he began to think she was clinically depressed.

He was concerned about the addictive effects of T.V. on its viewers. He even found himself subject to its wiles, and he resented it. As far as he was concerned television was just a substitute (and a bad one, at that) for more important forms of communication like the written word. He knew that where there was a television

178

The Muttering Retreats

set, there were people who weren't reading, which he saw as a personal affront, even though he knew that most T.V. watchers would probably never read any of his stuff. What he disliked most was the hypnotic effect television seemed to have on its victims. It was like a twentieth century Circe or Siren, enchanting modern-day Odysseuses into docility as they travel life's highway.

Holdorff had to admit that one of his best poems, a parody of both content and structure, was about how television mesmerizes his protagonist, a young man who believes what he sees on television, especially the commercials. He'd grown up in an orphanage in the Midwest and gone to a junior college before moving to Los Angeles where he gets a job as an operations officer trainee in a bank. When he's diagnosed with a terminal illness, he tries to make some sense of his life. It's then that he realizes he doesn't have much of a life. He has no identity. Everything he is has come from television. It's his moment of truth. He realizes what a sham his life has been. The poem ends when the young man dies alone on a Monday afternoon in an anonymous, deserted city park. His last dying gesture is to try to scratch his name into a rock with the ninety-nine cent penknife he'd seen advertised on a Saturday afternoon T.V. show.

Holdorff thought it was one of his best works of the 'sixties. Twenty-two manuscript pages of heroic couplets interspersed with Homeric epithets and epic similes. It was the longest sustained rap he'd ever written. He learned the age-old lesson once again: comedy and satire are the hardest things to write and the hardest to act. Somehow, even after he was done and was pleased with the finished product (he hated it when anyone referred to poetry as a product), he still wasn't satisfied with those similes. They seemed too elaborate for what was obviously a simple-minded black comedy. In the final analysis, he thought the triviality of consumer America was not really fit subject matter for an epic comedy. Nevertheless, he saw the madness that seemed to be engulfing the world around him. The poems were his island away from it, and that's also what they were really about.

Holdorff could see that not all television was bad. Every once in a while a nugget would sparkle in the wasteland. "Your Show of Shows" was one such nugget. He liked the writing on one of the shows so much that he waited for the end credits to see who the writers were. At the time he didn't think anything of it when

The Muttering Retreats

Mel Brooks's name appeared among the writers, but years later when he saw *Blazing Saddles*, he'd think back to those days when Brooks was writing for Sid Caesar and how funny the writing had been.

He liked Edward R. Murrow for his in-depth news coverage. When he could, he watched the Friday night fight, "brought to you by Gillette Blueblades, for the quickest, slickest shave of all. Look sharp and be on the ball...." He'd even seen an episode or two of *Maverick*, mostly because he thought James Garner was a good actor. In the end, he had to admit that there were some worthwhile shows on the boob tube. And there was plenty of work to go around for writers, directors, actors and crew. It wasn't all bad.

And that's another reason why Holdorff was moved to pride over his son. As H.H. got older, he didn't emulate his mother when it came to watching television. She'd watch anything. He watched a few select shows. Holdorff was always pleasantly surprised at how perceptive, discerning and selective H.H. was. He certainly had more on the ball that way than either his mother or his father. And, to his mother's credit, she wouldn't allow him to watch some of the stuff she and her mother watched.

He'd check out the game of the week on Saturday, but not every Saturday. He liked to watch "The Flintstones" and "Soupy Sales" after school, but not every day. Evenings, he only cared about "The Andy Griffith Show." He'd have nothing to do with Saturday morning cartoons.

On Friday nights when Holdorff went to pick H.H. up, the T.V. would invariably be on and his ex-wife and her mother would be watching some insipid situation comedy or western drama, but not H.H. He'd be in his room playing with his baseball cards or reading. Holdorff was proud to see that H.H. preferred books to television.

One Friday evening he went to pick the boy up for the weekend (Holdorff and Blake were taking him to the San Diego Zoo the next day), and when he entered the house, that unnatural sound of the television greeted him. Those abnormal sounding speaker-voices didn't sound human or animal to Holdorff. He thought even the human voice filtered through the electronic voice box didn't sound human. The picture shed a leaden blue hue throughout the room, which seemed to blunt and deaden everything it touched. A commercial was blaring out of the one-eyed monster. His ex-wife and ex-mother-in-law were watching from the couch. They both offered him a seat, but he declined.

"I've got a million things to do to get ready for the trip south tomorrow," he said moving off to H.H.'s room. As he did so, the bedroom door opened and H.H. came running out to greet him.

"Hey, Pop!"

They were going to San Diego by train. Holdorff had taken this trip when he was a kid. He'd gone with a group of newspaper boys who'd won it because they'd sold a certain number of subscriptions. It was one of the few childhood experiences that he could remember, and coincidentally it was one of the happier events of his youth. So, he decided to treat his son to the same happy experience. The other time he took the same train trip was when he'd left Los Angeles for boot camp in San Diego. This was going to be a big weekend for both of them; he was excited, and he knew H.H. was, too.

"Hey, pal, how you doin'?" Holdorff asked.

"C'm'ere an' take a look at the Jim Fregosi an' Bobby Knoop cards I j'st got."

He pulled him by the sleeve across the room to where he had a shoebox full of baseball

183

cards on his desk. He pulled out the two new cards and showed them to him.

"When did you get 'em?" Holdorff asked.

"Day before yesterday. Got this book, too."

He handed Holdorff a hardbound copy of a book called *Baseball's Greatest Players*. Each chapter was a profile of an individual player. Among them were Cy Young, Rogers Hornsby, Babe Ruth and Stan Musial.

"I already read the first three chapters. Boy, they sure had some great players back in the old times. Starts when they first started playin' baseball."

"Did you get to play any after school this week?"

"Johnny 'n' me played some catch, and hit some flies and grounders to each other. We both got good arms, but we can't throw any stuff, yet. His dad says we're too young to try an' throw curves and fast balls."

It pained Holdorff to hear this because his own knowledge of baseball was so limited. He wished he had some to share with his boy. But all he knew was how to write verse and pass tests in school.

The Muttering Retreats

"Well, that's good," he said trying to appear like he knew what he was talking about. "Don't do anything that's go'n'a hurt your arm. You wan'a be as good as Bob Gibson someday, right?"

"Yeah."

They left the ladies watching television and drove to Blake's house. Driving along Anaheim Street, they approached Recreation Park on the right, and H.H. suddenly said,

"Hey, Pop, that's Blair Field. Johnny's dad took us there to the last Dodgers and Angels spring training game a couple months ago. It's a neato ballpark just like the big leagues."

"Yeah, I know."

"Wow! You been there, too?"

"Just once," Holdorff lied. All he knew about it was what he'd seen from passing by. "Sounds like you guys had a swell time."

"Yeah."

They didn't say anymore for quite a while. Holdorff didn't know what to say. He wasn't a baseball fan, and he didn't know much about it. Even during World Series time, when televisions everywhere are tuned to it, bars are having betting pools on it, and students on campus are even tuned to it on portable radios, Holdorff couldn't drum up enough interest in it

185

to find out who was playing, not to mention what the score was. He couldn't even bring himself to read Jim Murray's column in the *Times*, even though he'd heard from people whose opinions he respected that Murray was an excellent writer. He'd read some Ring Lardner and thought it was humorous and cute, but ultimately he thought sporting events were about as apt a subject for serious writing as television.

They turned onto Pacific Coast Highway, and as they passed the Forty Niners, Holdorff saw the parking lot was filled with cars. Happy hour. As they passed the pumping oil wells on both sides of P.C.H., he thought about how someone once told him that the ground under them was lower than the highway because, as the oil was pumped out, the ground sank, but he found that hard to believe because he couldn't answer the question: why wouldn't the highway sink, too?

It was late spring and the orange haze of that season hung low over the marshland in front of them. The mornings were still a bit damp, but the late afternoons, like this one, were warm and lazy and comfortable.

"You looking forward to summer vacation, son?" Holdorff said to break the silence that hung between them. "Had enough school for one year?"

"Yeah, I can't wait. Johnny's dad's go'n'a get us into little league."

Again Holdorff felt the pain of his limited involvement with H.H. They only got together on the weekends, and because Holdorff was so busy with his own schoolwork, he could never find the time to meet with his son's teacher to discuss how he was doing. He'd been invited to an open house earlier in the year, but he couldn't make it because he'd had a big paper due the morning after, and, true to his record when it came to school work, he'd done nothing in preparation for it, so he spent the whole day of his son's open house doing the research and while the open house was going on, he was typing like a demon to finish it. He didn't get it done until midnight, and by that time, all he could think to do was go to the Forty Niners for a beer.

"'Nother reason I'm glad school's out is 'cause there's a bully keeps tryin' to pick a fight with me, and I don't wan'a fight 'im. Don't wan'a fight nobody. He's been after me all year. I'm sure glad summer's here 'cause then I don't have to see him all the time."

187

"Glad to see you're not reacting to the punk. Sluggin' him wouldn't do you any good."

"I'm scared to slug 'im. He'd j'st make mince meat outa' me. I'm real glad school's out."

"Yeah, but you're go'n'a have to deal with him again next year."

"Maybe he'll forget about it by then, or maybe he won't come back."

They stopped long enough at Blake's house to pick her up. They drove the short distance to Domenico's and parked on Pomona Avenue. At the corner liquor store, they picked up a newspaper for the movie listings. The restaurant was crowded with high school and college kids, so they had to wait a few minutes for a booth. When they got seated, Holdorff lit his pipe, and Blake browsed the entertainment section of the paper. They didn't have to look at the menu because they already knew they wanted a combination pizza without anchovies.

"*The Birds* is playing at the Circle drive-in," Blake said.

"Oh boy!" H.H. said. "I c'n tell Johnny I seen it. He already seen it."

"'Saw,' boy 'saw,'" Holdorff said good naturedly. "You got'a do better with the language."

The Muttering Retreats

They finished eating as twilight turned to night, so they hurried back to the car and headed to the drive-in. As they pulled into place and took the speaker off the hook, the credits were just finishing and the scene was the streets of San Francisco. As soon as they were settled, the boy said,

"Pop, I got'a go to the bathroom."

"Okay, I'll go with you," he replied to H.H. and then to Blake, "want anything from the snack bar?"

"How about a bag of buttered popcorn?"

"You got it. Be right back."

The next minute Holdorff and H.H. were walking across the graveled night to the building where there was a snack bar and a restroom. When they got into the central area between the snack bar on one side and the restrooms on the other, Holdorff said,

"You go ahead and go to the restroom, and I'll get some popcorn and sodas. It's okay, I'll be right over here."

Holdorff was responding to H.H.'s seeming hesitancy to go to the restroom by himself. His reassurance was all the boy needed, so Holdorff walked over to the snack bar keeping an occasional eye on the restroom door. He ordered a big bucket of buttered popcorn and three

Cokes, and when he turned around, his son was skipping across the floor toward him. There was a little round wet spot next to his fly. They walked together back to the car where they settled back to watch the movie.

H.H. fell asleep midway through, so Holdorff started the car and headed back to the Shore. He carried the boy, sound asleep, from the car into Blake's house and put him down in the spare bedroom. Then he joined her in the living room where they drank beers and watched the television news before going to bed themselves.

Fifteen

Holdorff, Blake and H.H. went to San Diego the next morning. They got an early start. Up at six, they'd had a breakfast of cold cereal and toast, coffee for the adults, milk for H.H. They caught the nine o'clock train out of Fullerton.

"You sleep okay?" Holdorff asked H.H. as they rolled south on the rails.

"Yeah. I fell asleep in the movie, huh Pop?"

"Yup. You passed out half way through it. We left early and went back to Blake's. You were done. It was okay, though. You didn't miss much. Movie wasn't very good. Wasn't hard to pull outa' there early. Had to get up early today, anyway."

"Yeah."

"We'll have loads of fun at the zoo, don't you think, H.H.?" Blake asked.

"Yeah, I heard it's real keen."

Blake had brought a deck of cards, so she and H.H. settled in and started playing War and Go Fish. Holdorff read a little from *Catch-22,* and watched the passing scenery out the train window. City turned to suburb to country and back to city.

They took a walk down to the club car, a long narrow space decorated in garish red and blue carpet. Blue vinyl-covered benches formed booths around scratched white Formica table tops. There was one unoccupied booth, so they sat there. Holdorff and Blake had coffee and his son had a Coke. As they watched the scenery pass by, they couldn't help but notice the people gathered at two tables on each side of the aisle having a party. One guy in the group was really loud. He'd had too much to drink for such an early hour. The two groups were obviously going to the races at Del Mar. Holdorff scrounged around in his jacket pockets looking for a match. He grasped a lapel in each hand and looked in the breast pockets. Only envelopes there. He got a book from the car attendant and stoked his pipe. They were coming up on San Juan Capistrano.

There was a television over the bar and the warm-up show for The Game of the Week was on. A group of couples on their way to Del

The Muttering Retreats

Mar were sitting at that end of the car reviewing the Daily Racing Form. They didn't look like high rollers. Maybe one or two of the men had played the ponies before, but for the most part they were middle class couples out for a day at the races. They were having a good time.

The train clacked along the rail south to San Juan Capistrano. A few people got off there. Tourists going to see the mission. They couldn't have been going to see the swallows return because that was a couple months ago. Then they were off again rolling past Camp Pendleton. A few marines got on at the gate. Five of them came into the club car. They were all spit-shined and barbered, and even though they were wearing civvies, Holdorff could tell they were jarheads. He looked at them and couldn't believe he once looked like that himself. Now, with collar length hair and full beard, he felt so far removed from that life that it almost seemed to have happened in a dream or didn't even happen at all.

He sipped his beer, and they watched the scene together. The baseball game was about to start. H.H. was taking an active interest in it. For one of the few times in his life, Holdorff was thankful that there was a television around.

"Who's playing?" he asked.

193

"Cubs 'n' Reds."

"You don't sound too excited."

"I like American League better'n National League. If it was Cardinals 'n' Reds, and Bob Gibson was pitching, I'd be more interested. This is okay, though. Rather watch this than nothin'."

"We'll just stay here and watch it then," Holdorff said. "That okay with you?" This to Blake.

"Sure."

When they got to Oceanside a few more Marines got on. After another stop at Encinitas, the train moved on to Del Mar, and the club car emptied. Holdorff, Blake and H.H. were left virtually alone (only a couple Marines remained) in the club car from Del Mar to San Diego. A few other people came and went, but it was nothing like the party atmosphere that had existed while the horse players were on board.

They pulled into the station in downtown San Diego and were off the train by twelve-thirty. They got on a bus that took them to the zoo. When they got there, they headed straight to the concession stand and got hot dogs and Cokes. Then they spent the next couple of hours walking around feeding peanuts to the animals. They stayed in the zoo till four-thirty. There was

194

The Muttering Retreats

still plenty of time before they had to be back to the train, so they went into downtown and had dinner at a Mexican restaurant.

The trip home was uneventful. H.H. slept most of the way as Blake rested her head on Holdorff's shoulder. The train ran a half hour late all the way. They didn't get back to Fullerton till almost ten-thirty. Then it was another half hour to Long Beach. Holdorff dropped Blake off at her place and took H.H. home. His mother and grandmother were watching television as they entered. It looked to Holdorff like the two women hadn't moved since he'd last seen them. H.H. went straight off to bed. After he'd kissed his dad goodnight and gone off to his room, his mother said to Holdorff,

"Really getting big, isn't he?"

Her sloe eyes still allured him, though he still felt bitterness about the bad marriage and the harrowing divorce.

"Yeah, he's quite a boy," Holdorff replied. "He's been a real gentleman the whole weekend. We watched a baseball game in the club car on the ride down, and he was explaining everything to me. I damn sure don't know anything about it on my own."

She laughed like she used to when they were first dating. The things he said never struck him as particularly funny, but she laughed at them and so did a lot of people, so they must have been funny. Her laugh, like her eyes, gave him a tingling sensation, as again he realized where he was and what he was doing.

"Well, I guess I should be getting back. Get some shuteye. Don't have to go back up to the city till tomorrow afternoon," he said after they'd run out of things to talk about.

His ex-mother-in-law sat on the couch, her eyes glued to the Louis Lomax late night call-in television show. His ex-wife walked with him out to the car.

"You know, he really misses you during the week. I'm glad you come to see him when you do," she said.

He couldn't tell if she was trying to make him feel guilty or just the opposite. One thing he did have a sense about was that right at that moment her attitude seemed to be the reverse of what it had been right after the divorce, and he didn't know if he could trust anything she said.

"Sometimes I really miss him too, but that's the way it goes. It's lonely living by yourself, but it's all right."

The Muttering Retreats

"You don't have to live by yourself, you know."

He didn't know what to make of that comment. Could she possibly think she could rekindle something between them? Nothing could be further from his mind. All he could say was,

"I've really got to be getting back."

He got into his car and headed over to Blake's place. She was already in bed and sound asleep. He was dead tired too, but not so tired that he couldn't write a couple poems, actually one poem and one song, on a couple of cancelled envelopes. He couldn't stop thinking about the conversation he'd had earlier with H.H.'s mom, and that's what he wrote about. It only took him fifteen minutes to write them. After he'd finished the writing, he sat down at Blake's typewriter and transcribed the two pieces.

Remembering Hurts too Much

It saddens me remembering the walk we took
　　that night.
The plans we made, though impossible seemed
　　so right.
I can't remember where we were heading,
Heartbreak Hotel or someplace I'm more

Jerome Arthur
dreading.

(Refrain)
It's hard to forget that we ever did touch,
'Cause remembering it hurts oh so much.

Wiling away days on the beach, browning under
the hot sun,
We stopped long enough to make love and have
some fun.
What a good life we had; it seems so long ago.
Now that it's over, I realize it was just another
show. (Refrain)

I'm movin' on down the long, lonesome road
I'm done a-carrying this heavy load.
I know so well that nothin' lasts forever,
So I'm just a-go'n'a keep on keepin' on till
whenever. (Refrain)

He zipped that one out of the typewriter and put
in another blank sheet.

When Yuh Go'n'a Leave

When yuh go'n'a leave
Me alone to retrieve
My own fate?
I don't need no date
With no one who
Can only say adieu
As easily as
Hello and has

The Muttering Retreats

The nerve to say,
"I won't even lay
In bed with other
Lovers." I smother
Just thinking that I
Could not dare pry
You away from that life
And make you my wife,
But that's symbolic;
It's too bucolic
For the likes of you,
A real swinger who
Just won't settle down
And quit runnin' 'round.
I gave myself credit,
But indeed you said it;
There would only be me,
And I couldn't see
It would never happen.
Now I only laugh and
Remember the good times
And put them in rhymes.

He folded the four sheets, two originals and two carbon copies, stuffed them and the envelopes with the rough drafts into the breast pocket of his jacket, brushed his teeth, and climbed into the sack next to Blake. He slept till ten o'clock the next morning and got back on the road to Los Angeles early in the afternoon.

Sixteen

Holdorff couldn't believe his ears.

"Ever notice how sex is the first thing to go when that initial glow wears off a relationship or marriage? We've only been married for a year and a half, and my spouse has already lost interest in nooky. Too bad, 'cause for me that's one of the most important parts, if not *the* most important part, of a relationship. My spouse says I'm a nymphomaniac. I just like to screw. I'm hot all the time, and he's indifferent. I was even hotter the summer after my first year of college. Must've screwed fifty guys."

This was the first time they had lunch together. They'd met at the beginning of this the winter quarter in an American novel class he was auditing. For her it was an elective. Her major was Spanish lit. It was Holdorff's second quarter of auditing. He was sitting next to her on the first day of class, but they didn't talk until twenty minutes after the class was over when they were on the bus coming down off the hill into town.

It was on that bus ride that he learned that she was twenty-two years old and already a year into her second marriage. She struck up a conversation with him out of the blue. And that was how it started. They sat together on the bus ride back to town for the rest of that quarter. By mid quarter, they were having lunch together and she was telling him about her voracious sexual appetite.

"You realize don't you that our culture is in the minority when it comes to the taboo against extramarital sex. You ever take an anthropology class?"

"Nope," he said.

"One of the things I learned was that there are many cultures on this planet that are not monogamous. In fact with some cultures, like the indigenous peoples in the north pole for example, it's a compliment when one man offers his wife to another man, and if the recipient doesn't accept, he's insulting the giver."

"Oh yeah," he said. "The custom in most of Central and South America and some of Europe is that married men have mistresses. Ever see *Divorce Italian Style*?"

"Yes. Great movie! It's a fact of life in all Latin cultures. I don't understand the Anglo-Christian concept of monogamy."

She did that little curl up of her lower lip that so captivated him. He didn't quite know what to make of her. He'd heard this line before, but never from a woman. He'd heard it often enough from guys like Novak. She went on.

"In fact, the idea of men and women being faithful quote/unquote to each other for the rest of their lives is ridiculous. A bit much to expect of anybody. People are attracted to each other. Just because you're married doesn't change that. My friends can't believe it when I talk this way."

Holdorff could surely relate to that.

"I was a virgin all through high school, a model student with a 4.0 G.P.A. I didn't have my first sexual experience until I went away to college, and after that I couldn't get enough. I was doing it so much that sometimes it was four nights, five guys."

"How does your "spouse" feel about all this?"

"He knows what he has."

"Does he?"

"He won't leave."

The Muttering Retreats

Holdorff was ten years older than she was, not quite the requisite number, but he still thought of her as the next generation, and he had to admit from time to time that he didn't understand it. He remembered something old Doc Powers once said when he was lecturing on the virgin goddess Artemis in world lit.

"Girls are giving it up earlier and earlier. These days I imagine the average age is probably about sixteen."

The world was changing so rapidly for Holdorff that sometimes he had trouble keeping up. Students were shutting down universities in protest of the Vietnam War. They wanted to "make love not war," and that idea was catching on. The protesters were rejecting their parents' values, and that included their ideas about love and war.

He'd come across some strange points of view in his travels, and this had to be one of the strangest, so if he sounded cynical, it was only because he was surprised when he heard it. Once again he was asking himself who he was to be surprised, and who cared anyway since he could see pretty plainly that it wouldn't be too long before he'd have her in bed in his little cottage.

Jerome Arthur

But the more he thought about that, the less inclined he was to take her to his place because he wasn't a tidy housekeeper. She was surprisingly middle class and clean cut. Unlike many of the other U.C. Santa Cruz coeds he'd come in contact with, she shaved her legs and armpits, and although she wore jeans like the others, unlike many of the others, her jeans were clean. He appreciated that, especially since he equated dirty jeans with a scroungy person, and that was one thing he could not tolerate. His house was messy, but he was personally tidy. If he was in a classroom and he could smell somebody's B.O., he'd very bluntly say, "you stink" to the offender and get up and leave the room. A couple times he even said it to teachers. He kept a squalid house (it looked like an artist's loft), but his personal hygiene was always respectable, even as he approached middle age and after having lived so long alone.

"I could have sex twice a day seven days a week. I can't believe how my spouse can go without it for two or three weeks at a time. What am I supposed to do when he's not in the mood? I've got'a have it. I didn't get any when I was in high school, but once I found out how it is, I started doing it all the time, and really, what better way to spend my time? It feels good and it's good exercise. I got laid more when I was single than I ever have since I've been married."

Holdorff could only nod his head. He began to get that aching feeling in his chest, that feeling that comes when you know you're going to enjoy the pleasures of love making with a pretty woman. It was the same feeling he experienced just before making love with his ex-wife the first time. He'd also had it with Blake in Las Vegas. About the only time he hadn't experienced it was the first time, which was when he was a teenager, and that was probably because he was so young and he didn't really know what was happening. But he did remember feeling it right afterwards when he and the young woman (he couldn't even remember her name, and when he was young, he swore he'd never forget it) went their separate ways.

Holdorff was always somewhat of a romantic, and it wasn't immediately apparent to those he dealt with. He worked at putting up a façade. In truth, although he was a rational thinker, or at least he saw himself as such, he couldn't figure out why he became so emotionally involved with the few women whom he'd made love to. It was always the same. He'd make love to a woman, and then he couldn't get her out of his mind for weeks after the event.

And it always started with a mournful, aching feeling in his chest, the feeling described by romantics from John Keats to Hank Williams.

She suggested they take a walk along the beach. They'd picked up burritos at a Mexican restaurant near the wharf and had eaten them on the sea wall next to the Dream Inn. They walked through the soft dry sand toward the surf. When they got to the wet compacted sand that marked the high tide, they turned and walked along the shoreline toward the cliff. He was at a total loss for words at the moment, and he really hoped that the uneasiness, the uncertainty he was feeling, was going unnoticed. She seemed to be in complete control of herself, but he was sure she was feeling just as uncertain as he was and was hiding it just as he was.

"We're getting down to the wire, 'far as the quarter goes," he finally said.

"Less than a month left."

"What're yuh takin' spring quarter?"

"Only taking one class. Spanish. Think I'm taking some time off after that. I'm doing all right as far as my studies go. I just want to go to work for a while. Make some money. Finish school later."

They walked along the beach, and he tried to think of a way to get the conversation back to sex without sounding overly eager. He wanted to make love to her, but he wanted to be cool about it. Then suddenly he realized that he didn't have to direct anything.

"We ought to do this again soon, only next time skip the lunch. Do something else," she suggested.

This was the break he'd been waiting for. His heart jumped and he could feel his mouth getting dry. He'd been smoking his pipe off and on as they walked. Now he put it into the pocket of his rumpled corduroy jacket.

"Okay with me. How 'bout next week?"

His response didn't sound very enthusiastic, but his heartbeat picked up, and he could tell that she was as excited as he was. That ancient game was being played out, and all the emotional attachments that go with it were coming into play.

"Okay," she said. "What day?"

"I don't know. How 'bout one of the days you don't have class? I mean, we should probably plan it for when you're not in class?"

"So the class meets Monday, Wednesday and Friday. Let's plan on next Tuesday. The question is where?"

"Guess we could go to my place. Got'a clean it up, though. In fact, I'd say let's go there this afternoon, but the place is a shambles."

"No. Not this afternoon. I have to be back home at three o'clock. I don't want our first time to be a quickie. Let's take it slow. I've already waited six weeks; I can wait for one more."

"You can?"

"Of course." Her response flattered him. "I don't mind a little clutter. Just make sure the bed is made."

"How can you get time away from your spouse?"

"That's why we have to do it during the week 'cause that's when he works."

"Okay, then. What time Tuesday?"

"I could be at your place by eleven-thirty."

"Okay. So what kind of an arrangement you guys got, anyway? Does he go out with other women?"

"He's free to, but I don't think he does. In fact, he's told me there's a young woman where he works who has a crush on him. I told him to go ahead and go out with her."

Holdorff was trying to understand this in his own mind. He thought he'd seen just about everything, but this arrangement was a new one on him. Didn't she have any feelings of jealousy? And what about her old man? What kind of guy didn't mind if his wife was out getting laid by every Tom, Dick and Harry she met? There's not much anybody can do about it when it happens. Either member of any couple can screw around with someone else and keep it completely secret. It happens all the time. He just couldn't imagine himself being married to someone he knew was going to bed with different guys all the time. But apparently (at least according to her) her husband knew all about it and wasn't concerned. If he were to believe her, she'd spend an afternoon in a motel room with one of her "dates" and then go home and tell her spouse all about it. Holdorff just couldn't believe it.

"It's time for me to be getting back to the valley. I belong to this woman's club up there, and I'm meeting the president at three. She and I are going to look at a hall to rent for the political forum we're having at our next meeting."

Holdorff's Sedan Delivery was twenty-two years old by now, so he didn't drive it much. The bus system had a convenient route to the university and downtown, so that's how he got around. He'd walked to the restaurant and met the woman there for the lunch date. She drove out West Cliff Drive and dropped him off at his garret. When they parted, he leaned over from the shotgun seat of her Datsun and French kissed her. As he was doing it, he gently fondled her breast. She, in her turn, massaged his beard with her left hand and returned the kiss with equal passion. Then she drove off leaving him standing on the curb in front of his house. He went in, sat down at his typewriter and wrote a song:

Rayaya, the Rock 'n' Roll Queen

The place was shut down when she came in,
And just her presence opened it up again.
She walked through the door, book balanced on
    her head,
In her hand a spray of roses white and red.
There was no book anywhere that could tell
The story of Rayaya, the Rock 'n' Roll Queen.

"Why the book on your head," I said.
"You learnin' to model to make some bread?"
But she only smiled a knowing smile
And hung around for just a little while.
Yeah, she would hang around to begin
The tale of Rayaya, the Rock 'n' Roll Queen.

"I'm already a model," was her reply,

The Muttering Retreats

And it wasn't for me to question why.
Then when she asked, "You got a vase?"
I knew she saw the confusion in my face.
Nothing was beyond the reach of
Coffee-colored Rayaya the Rock 'n' Roll Queen.

"Yuh mean ye're leavin' them with me?"
I didn't need to ask; I could clearly see.
"No question, no question," was her response.
In a little while, would she satisfy my wants?
The only thing in question was,
Could she, Rayaya the Rock 'n' Roll Queen.

I found a jar in the next room,
And in it she placed the flowers abloom.
Since they were hers to give to me,
I let her put them where they would be.
And that's when she told me that
Her name was Rayaya, the Rock 'n' Roll Queen.

"Do you live somewhere around here?"
I shouldn't have asked, it was clear.
"I live everywhere," she smiled,
That's when I knew to hang with her'd be wild.
'Cause I learned quick not to evade
The power of Rayaya, the Rock 'n' Roll Queen.

As she set the roses on the table,
I could see she had legs like Betty Grable.
Suddenly she was on her way to the door,
But I wanted her to stay for a while more.
But there wouldn't be any doors
Holding back Rayaya, the Rock 'n' Roll Queen.

211

Jerome Arthur

"Ye're not leavin' so soon, are you?"
I hoped she'd stay till the morning dew,
But she put her book back on her head,
And moved on to the door instead.
There was no turning back for
Coffee-colored Rayaya, the Rock 'n' Roll Queen

But before she got away, I got a hug
That was as delightful as a ladybug.
As her lips brushed the side of my face,
I was consumed in her embrace.
I'm sure I wasn't the only one to be
Held in the arms of Rayaya, the Rock 'n' Roll
        Queen.

Then I whispered it in her ear,
Asked her if she was ever coming back here,
But she only smiled that knowing smile
That said she'd not come back for a while.
Though it migh's well have been, it wasn't
The last of Rayaya, the Rock 'n' Roll Queen.

But that's okay with me now,
Though I really do have to allow
That I waited hopefully for her return.
It's probably better; it just wasn't my turn.
It was a brief encounter, but I
Still think of Rayaya, the Rock 'n' Roll Queen.

Seventeen

Holdorff saw her the following Monday after her class. She pulled up in front of his apartment at eleven-thirty. He'd spent the morning vacuuming and cleaning. The night before on his way home from the Catalyst, he'd stopped at Bonesio's on Pacific Avenue and bought a half gallon of Cribari rosé. The only glasses he had around the house were jelly jars. He thought about buying a couple of wine glasses for the date, but he never got around to it, and he couldn't really afford it, anyway. Besides, he didn't know if this was going to be a one-time-shot or if he would see her again. He was loading his pipe when she knocked.

"How's it goin'?" he asked as he opened the door.

"A lot better now," she said, moving in and closing the door behind her. She embraced him and kissed him passionately.

"Whoa," he said when she finally let go of him.

They undressed each other and were in bed making love within five minutes. After the climax they lay spent and swooning in each other's arms.

"Are you going to keep on auditing classes?"

"Don't know, yet. Gettin' tired a' doin' it. Too much repetition."

He really didn't want to talk about academia, especially his present affiliation (or lack thereof) with it. Of late he felt out of place on campus. Whenever the people there (students and teachers) found out what he was doing, they viewed him with suspicion from then on. He didn't have friends at this campus like he'd had at Long Beach, S.D.U.N., and U.S.C., except, of course, this woman he was with now. And the only reason he was with her was because *she* went after *him*. His friends here were for the most part non-university people, guys he'd met at the Bei's and the Asti. The university people made it abundantly clear to Holdorff that they were in and he was out. As far as they were concerned, he was just another campus bum.

But he couldn't stop himself from going up there and just hanging around; sit in on a

The Muttering Retreats

class here and there. Campus was his security blanket. When he was on a campus, in a classroom, hanging around with people who shared his interest in literature, he was at home. So he swallowed his pride and went on campus as a non-student and watched and listened and was amused by what he saw and heard. He really liked the school. The physical location was beautiful, situated in a redwood forest on the side of a mountain with sweeping views of Monterey Bay and the Pacific Ocean.

The natural beauty of the campus was one thing; the curriculum and general educational philosophy was something else. Except in the sciences and math, there were no letter grades. Teachers gave their students what they called narrative evaluations. Holdorff thought it was an easy grading system, which, along with the setting, probably explained its popularity and why it was such a tough institution to get into. It seems more people wanted to go there than they had openings for in either the graduate or undergraduate program. The school was only in its sixth year of operation. It was the perfect antithesis to the large degree factories that Long Beach, S.D.U.N. (later, Nevada Southern University, and now U.N.L.V.), and U.S.C. had become. Because it was so small, you didn't hear a lot about any protests against the Vietnam war or in support of the civil rights movement, like what was going on at Berkeley in 'sixty-four and Columbia in 'sixty-eight. He'd always agreed with many of the students' gripes, but he didn't condone shutting down classes.

He lived in Santa Cruz during the transition years. When he first arrived, it was clearly a retirement/resort community. Now it was rapidly becoming a university town, resulting in the growth of a large transient segment of the population year-round. In pre university days, the transient population was tourists who only came in the summer when Santa Cruz was a small seaside resort and the only thing to recommend it was the Giant Dipper and other amusements at the Boardwalk.

And with the university came that weird transient element characteristic of many other university towns, the radical fringe of legitimate communists, socialists and other assorted left wing types, followed by the screwballs, who are neither left nor right, just goofy people engaged in bizarre behavior. Some people might even classify Holdorff in this group. Indeed, he was a transient, but by Santa Cruz standards, he was too much in the American mainstream to be

The Muttering Retreats

thought of as living a gypsy or bohemian life-style.

Thus, his attraction to this average American woman lying next to him. She was not the typical U.C.S.C. student. Apart from her promiscuity, she was very middle class. She was open, talkative and direct. By contrast his ex-wife was introverted, taciturn and mysterious. Her strong suit was her sloe-eyed beauty. He had to admit there weren't many women more beautiful than she was. Neither this woman nor Blake came close to his ex-wife when it came to shear physical beauty, but, as he was getting older, he was learning that personality, too, has a lot to do with beauty.

He was also finding out that many gorgeous women were only interested in the tease, and this was not true of the woman he was lying next to. With her everything was right out front. There was no tease. *She* came after *him*, apparently with only one thing in mind, and he was receptive, but overly self-conscious. He hadn't wanted to appear too eager. And now with her lying naked next to him, all of it initiated by her, he felt foolish for having worried about that. Looking at her profile, he noticed a curious smile in her eyes.

"What's with the grin?" he asked.

"Just thinking. It's been two years since I've done something like this. Met a guy at his place or in a motel room. Gotten laid. Afternoon delight."

He liked how this kind of conversation with a woman made him feel. He'd certainly had his share of guilt feelings through his youth, as probably most Americans growing up at that time did, but he'd gotten over them, and now he was glad he was still of an age that he could be a part of what would later be referred to as the sexual revolution. However, he still had some problems in that regard. It's not that he wasn't physically attractive to a lot of women. His direct approach was his downfall. He found that women wanted to be romanced; in other words, "bull-shitted," and he didn't want to go to the trouble. He probably could have been a good man for any number of them, but he never got past the part where he had to be honest with them.

He thought he was honest, but then he couldn't be sure, since he wasn't the best judge of his own feelings. Without a doubt, Holdorff's biggest problem was that he had to be himself, and most of the women he met wanted him to be someone else. Not this one. She didn't seem to care what he said or did, just as long as he bed-

The Muttering Retreats

ded her. When he was married, it was a constant battle to get sex. What he was doing now was great fun, and he was happy someone was pursuing him for a change. He sucked it for all he could get, enjoying all those melancholy feelings that come with a developing relationship.

Three hours after they'd started, they dragged themselves out of bed, took showers and sat in the living room of his little ramshackle apartment sipping wine from jelly jars. His place was above a garage behind a house on a street that was paved, but had potholes and no sidewalks. It fit his lifestyle. The stacks of poems he'd written over the last sixteen years sat on two shelves of the refrigerator. Next to the stacks was half a six-pack of beer. A saucepan half filled with water stood on one of the back burners of the stove. Next to it on the counter was a jar of instant coffee. The old box-shaped, antique Underwood he'd bought used when he started out at Long Beach City College was on the table next to two canceled envelopes with notes scribbled on them. The outbox was on the other side with carbon copies of six songs on top of about a hundred poems (enough to start thinking about trying to get them published). There was an unfinished poem in the typewriter carriage.

"I need to use the restroom," she said when she finished her wine.

"Go ahead."

"This is a cute place," she said as she came out of the bathroom. "How long did you say you've been living here?"

"A couple years. Only place I've ever had since I've been in Santa Cruz. And now I don't even know why I moved here."

"Why do you *think* you moved here?"

"Good question. I wanted to go to graduate school up at the U. I liked the town from the first time I laid eyes on it. It's like how I imagine Long Beach must've looked maybe fifty years ago. But the main reason was to break into the academic community here. Only thing I've ever known for the last fifteen years or so. I've done some other things along the way, like pushing produce and dealing twenty-one, but those were both boring. I never get tired of reading good lit. and writing about it and discussing it."

While she was in the restroom, he'd refilled her wine glass.

"C'm'on in here while I finish this poem I started earlier," he said, directing her to the table.

The Muttering Retreats

He sat down in front of the Underwood; she sat in the chair opposite. He looked at the unfinished poem in the typewriter carriage. He'd started it that morning in anticipation of this meeting with her. After the time they'd had together, he was suddenly inspired to finish it, and within a couple of minutes, he was clattering out the ending. When he was done, he zipped it out of the carriage and handed the carbon to her.

Stark Raving

We got into the tub
And I began to rub
Your beautiful tattoo.
It was all I could do.

We settled in
And tried to win
Each other's trust
Not being nonplussed.

Was the first I learned
That you really yearned
For a life quite different
Than I could present.

You came into my life—
Pierced my heart with your knife.
We stayed in the tub

And continued to scrub.

"I like it," she said.

"Keep it. I wrote it for you."

"Really? How sweet! When did you start it?"

"This morning. Thinking about our date."

"You sure you want me to have it?"

"Of course. Here, let me sign it. If you don't take it, it'll just end up in some agent's or publisher's trash can. The original's going in the reefer."

"What?"

"C'm'ere," he said, as he walked over to the refrigerator and opened the door. He put the original of the poem on top of the stack.

She looked in and saw the small stack of loose sheets on top of three bound bundles.

"Oh my God! What have we here?"

"Insurance," he replied.

He opened the door wide so she could see that the bundles made two stacks a foot high each. She was astonished at their size.

"You've done a lot of work here, but why do you keep them in the refrigerator?"

"Like I said, insurance. If this house ever burns down, my poems won't burn with it."

The Muttering Retreats

She fingered the stack and shook her head.

"Probably wouldn't burn anyway," she said. "Edges might get singed a little, but that's about all. I don't think any air could possibly get in there, and you need oxygen to burn anything. How come it's all tied up like that?"

"Bundles represent different stages of my writing. Bottom half the bundle on the left is my work from the beginning when I was a sailor in San Francisco till I left Long Beach for Las Vegas. Top half of the bundle's my Vegas period. Bundle on the right is my work from when I got back to Long Beach until I left Southern Cal. The loose ones on top are what I've done since I've been in Santa Cruz."

"It seems like such a waste to have them bundled up like that and hidden away in the refrigerator. You don't want to get them published?"

"Been trying to get 'em published from the beginning. No luck. Take that back. I actually got two of 'em published in little magazines, but all I got for my trouble was thirty copies of each. No big deal. Stuff in the outbox is ready to go out right now. Nothin' comes a' that, it's okay. What's most important is getting it down, freezing a moment in time until it crystallizes. And I don't need an editor in a cubicle in a skyscraper in some distant land who doesn't even read it to grant or deny me that. If, after I read it, I feel like I've captured that moment, that's all *I* need."

He was talking about what he knew best so he was animated and alive with enthusiasm. He thought if only the people at U.C.S.C. could see him now. They'd have to be impressed with his knowledge and his skill at conveying it. The woman he was with was certainly impressed. He could tell that much, even though he was never sure what her reactions to him were otherwise.

From a drawer next to the sink, he took a pair of scissors and cut the twine that was holding the Las Vegas bundle. This, he thought, was some of his best work. At the time he was still young enough to have a sense of idealism, but he'd surpassed his earlier naïveté to the degree that his poems showed sensitivity with only a tinge of sarcasm in the tone. His later work became so sardonic that people often misconstrued his intent and accused him of being too negative. But the Las Vegas poems were a perfect balance between his earlier idealism and his cynicism later on.

"Here, read this one," he said after shuffling through the pile and finding one that looked good. When he was in Las Vegas, he'd try to get out on the desert at sunrise as much as he could. He'd try to write a poem describing what he saw. This was one of those poems. He watched her eyes to see her reaction as she read.

Sunshine in Every Drop

I awoke to the rain
And could feel the strain
Of its hard drumming
Like a guitar strumming
Music to my ears.
Suddenly my fears
Had all disappeared
Like the sky had cleared.
A new day was shining;
It had a gold lining.
The rain didn't stop,
Sunshine in every drop.

"That's good," she said enthusiastically when she finished. "Those images are so beautiful. I wish I could write like that."

"You want a copy?" he asked, taking it from her and walking over to the typewriter. He slipped a clean sheet of paper in the carriage and clattered away for about five minutes. When he stopped typing, he zipped the finished copy out of the carriage and signed it above where he'd

225

typed his name and the date it was originally written. "There's a signed copy for you. If you sell it, be sure to send me the royalties."

"It's really great that you can write like this. I can't write fiction at all. Never could. I can only study it."

"But you know how to write," he said. "As cynical as I am, I can't believe you had 4.0 out of high school and you've gotten through a couple years of college without knowing how to write. And every form of writing has its place, even, as much as I hate to admit it, literary criticism, and that's basically what you're doing in research papers that you write in your classes."

"I haven't really gotten so far in college. I'm barely finishing up my second year, and that was after taking a year off after my first year. Now I'm thinking about taking some time off again. As far as the stuff I'm writing now, it may have its place, but it sure is boring. As interesting as fiction is to read, it must be fun to write, but I just can't do it. Somehow the guidelines seem too loose. I need structure."

"Sounds to me like you're contradicting yourself. Not long ago you said that the world is in a constant state of flux and there is no reality. So why not just apply that to your writing and you'll have fiction, and maybe good fiction at that."

"I don't know. You make it sound so easy. I can handle the writing part of it; I just couldn't think up any good stories."

"Why not? You've had a lot of different relationships. You could write about your sexual experience. The story you've been telling me would make great reading. All you've got'a do is do it. It's all in your values. You're going to school and writing all that required bullshit because you want to. If you know how to write and you want to, you can write anything, even fiction."

She didn't seem to be listening to him anymore. She seemed distracted, suddenly out of sorts, as though she didn't want any of his two-bit advice. Her look was saying, "I don't want to hear this. I know what I want and don't want, and I can figure it out myself." He wouldn't see that look on her face enough times to know what she really meant by it. In fact, she was so self-possessed and confident that he was beginning to feel uneasy with her.

His feelings toward her were rife with ambiguity. On the one hand he had a physical desire to have sex with her, while at the same time her strong personality was beginning to

227

repel him. So he decided to succumb to his physical instincts. It wasn't worth getting into an argument over. He said no more about it. He put the original copy of the poem back in the middle of the stack where it came from, and tied it back up into a bundle. He stacked the two bundles back in the refrigerator and sat down in the chair by the typewriter. She sat down in the other chair. The scene was a tableau, broken only by Holdorff when he raised his wine to his lips and took a sip.

"So, when do you wan'a do this again?"

"Well, how about Tuesday the sixth? Two weeks from tomorrow. I can't see you a week from tomorrow because I have a lunch date with two guys in Palo Alto. Can you believe it? I'm going all the way to Palo Alto just for lunch. These two guys and I did this crazy thing one time, and we've celebrated the event every year since by having lunch together."

"Two weeks'd be great. You wan'a come over here again?"

"That'll be fine," she said as she headed toward the door.

He came up beside her, put his arm over her shoulder and kissed her. She fell into his arms and stroked his beard. Just when he

228

thought he wouldn't have to wait two weeks, she whispered in his ear,

"We can't do this now. I have to be going. I have a few things to do before my spouse gets home."

"Okay," he said, as he walked her to her car.

Eighteen

Holdorff answered the door. She was standing on the porch holding a bottle of Christian Brothers zinfandel. She was wearing makeup, a svelte red dress and black high heel shoes. He took the wine and stood aside so that she could enter before him. The cottage was spotless. He'd cleaned all morning. He'd scoured the bathroom and washed the sheets. He made the bed up as smoothly as when he was in boot camp. He vacuumed the rug. The two wine glasses he'd bought were sitting on the table behind the Underwood.

"Wow! Don't you look good? Wha'da you tell your spouse when you go out dressed like that?"

"He works over the hill. He's gone by six-thirty. Doesn't get home till quarter to six at night."

"How late can you stay here?"

The Muttering Retreats

"Till four o'clock. We can screw till three-fifteen."

They moved a bit slower this time. He wondered why they were doing all this talking as he scrounged around in a drawer for a cork-screw. When he found one, he uncorked the bottle and poured two glasses. He handed one to her, and they held them up and toasted.

"Cheers."

"Cheers. You bought wine glasses," she said after she took a sip. "What happened to the jelly jars? They were kinda' cute."

They set their glasses on the table and fell into a deep kiss. And for the second time in as many weeks, they were in bed making passionate love, but this time was different. He wasn't sure if he liked the pornographic-movie-star roll she'd taken on. He liked her better as a middle class housewife. Nonetheless, Holdorff thought the sex was pretty damn good either way. They spent a full three hours in bed, sips of wine intermingled with four ejaculations and five orgasms. She *was* hot! The conversation centered on themselves and each other.

Mellowed by the wine, they passed a delightful afternoon together, and as the time for parting approached, Holdorff didn't want to let her go. He was logical enough to know that the time would come when he wouldn't want to see her at all, but emotionally at this moment, he had this forever feeling, and he liked it. He dragged himself out of the bed right behind her. As he washed the afternoon's aroma from his beard, she took a shower. It wouldn't have been a good idea for her to go home to her spouse smelling like she'd spent the afternoon turning tricks.

"I could do this every week," she said as she fastened the hook on her brassiere. "In fact, I could get laid twice a day. I wish my spouse was a little more interested in sex."

"I could do it every week, too. Way I feel, I could do it again right now and tonight and tomorrow, but you have a spouse to get home to."

"Yes, I do."

It was over as quickly as it had started. She was out the door and Holdorff was alone once again in his clean but sex-smelling garret. He sat down at the typewriter, but for reasons he didn't know, he couldn't write. Instead, his thoughts wended their way back to the woman he'd spent the day with. He couldn't get her out of his mind so he sat hunched over the type-writer, not writing a thing. He couldn't say why he didn't feel like writing about her.

The Muttering Retreats

It was like those other occasions when words failed him, but he'd try to write anyway. If he had trouble getting started, he'd jot down random rhymes. If that didn't stimulate him, he'd move on to famous quotes he attached particular significance to. If he got lucky, his thoughts would clear. Sometimes he'd get a good poem or two this way, and other times, like now, he'd get nothing.

He stood up and looked at the blank sheet of paper in the carriage. He'd expended himself with his afternoon playmate, and now he guessed he didn't have the necessary juices to fuel the creative effort. What he needed right now was an ice cold beer and a crowd, so he put his jacket on and went out the door. The Underwood was thus left alone in the house with the two clean, white, blank sheets of paper that sandwiched a carbon reaching out the backside of the carriage.

Holdorff climbed in behind the wheel of the Sedan Delivery and drove off toward downtown. He drove along West Cliff Drive out to Lighthouse Point. As he rounded the bend at the point, he saw an old man with hair as white as snow and a face as red as a fire engine leaning on the redwood railing that faced Its beach. He held a cigarette in his right hand. He raised it to his mouth and drew a couple times. It wasn't lit, so he didn't draw in any smoke. He held it out and looked at it, shook his head and put his hand back on the railing. He gazed at the horizon as Holdorff drove past.

There were no parking places on Front Street, so Holdorff drove down to Cooper Street, turned right and went over to Pacific Avenue. He took another right on Pacific and found a space just beyond County Bank. As he stepped out of the dusty Sedan Delivery lighting his pipe, he almost looked like Chaplin's little tramp in his rumpled, leather-elbowed corduroy jacket, stay-pressed trousers and dusty, tan suede desert boots.

As he walked the half block up to the Saint George, he passed Tom Scrivner playing his saw. When he first got to town, they were just beginning the renovation of this street. It was now the Pacific Garden Mall, not just Pacific Avenue. There were five guys hanging around by the Saint George entry. All had long hair and bizarre clothing. They had pierced ears and noses, and spangled and sequined jackets. He hurried past them as quickly as he could and into the lobby of the Saint George where their older broken-tooth counterparts were sitting in viscid, shiny old couches and easy chairs watching the television next to the fake fireplace.

He walked quickly around the fountain to the back door of the Catalyst. He entered the men's room on the left and stood at one of the huge old-fashioned waist-high porcelain urinals. Two guys with long hair, scruffy beards, hip-hugging bell-bottoms, and psychedelic tie-dye shirts were talking to each other in the mirrors above the row of sinks about some demonstration they'd been to over the weekend in San Francisco. End the draft, stop the war, some such thing. Holdorff couldn't make it out. He zipped his trousers up, washed his hands, and went out into the bar.

There was a good size crowd there for a Tuesday. End-of-the-work-day crowd, but a good mix. Men in business suits, probably lawyers, standing at the bar next to hippy types and university students. There were three bar stools not being used, so Holdorff took one and ordered a draft. It was just what he needed for his melancholy mood. He couldn't get his mind off the woman he'd spent the afternoon with. He couldn't believe she was as open with her spouse as she claimed. No man would continue living with a woman who admitted spending her afternoons in somebody else's room while he was at work. He might be able to take it for a while, but eventually the novelty would wear off and jealousy would set in. Even *her* jealousy emerged when she told Holdorff about a guy who quit seeing her because he threw his wife over for another one of his mistresses, not her. She was incensed when she found out what happened, and she made little effort to hide her anger.

"If he only knew how much of a crush I had on him," she told Holdorff.

He took this to mean that she wanted the guy to marry her instead of the other mistress. Indeed, what else could it be but jealousy of the other mistress, the lucky one who got the catch? Based on his two sexual encounters with her, his first thought was that the guy missed the boat. He even thought her spouse was lucky to have her, but then he immediately changed his mind and thought how unlucky he was.

...but what a good lay, he thought, and took a sip of his beer.

The more he tried to understand her, the more of an enigma she was to him. But then he wasn't sure he even understood himself. In fact, he was sure he didn't understand himself, so how could he possibly be expected to understand her? And that, he suddenly realized, was

The Muttering Retreats

at the bottom of all relationships between men and women. Try as they may, they couldn't understand each other simply because they didn't understand themselves, and perhaps never would. Only a most privileged few of this world understand themselves, and they seem to understand just about everything else in the universe as well, including the opposite sex.

He decided to go have a bite to eat, so he drained the beer from his glass, lit his pipe and headed back through the hotel. He drove to Tampico Kitchen on lower Pacific Avenue where he had enchiladas, beans and rice, and two bottles of Dos Equis, one while he waited, puffing on his pipe, for his order to be prepared, the second with his meal.

He was beginning to feel a buzz, but the food stalled it slightly, keeping him from getting wasted. He was consoled by the fact that his house would be clean and neat and comfortable when he got back there, and he could just flop into bed, alone. He paid the check and left a small tip.

His tips were small of late. Sometimes he wouldn't leave a tip at all simply because he didn't have the money. He still had his disability, but his G.I. benefits had run out at S.C. three years ago. The job market for pushing produce and pushing chalk in Santa Cruz wasn't good. He hadn't worked since he came to town, and since he was no longer a bona fide student, he had no scholarship, grant or loan money at his disposal. His only income was his Navy disability pension, which was really only a pittance compared to what he was used to. He'd had to curtail some of his comforts, things he'd taken for granted when he was at S.D.U.N., Long Beach State and U.S.C. He was even cutting back his consumption of beer and buying cheaper brands, and that was one of the hardest things for him to do. An ice-cold beer (or two or three) a day was one of his greatest pleasures. But now he was learning to cut back because of lack of funds.

He'd parked halfway between Tampico Kitchen and Bonesio's Liquors at the corner of Pacific and Laurel, so he took the short walk from the restaurant to the liquor store. Standing next to the liquor store doorway was a gray old man with no teeth and white hair to his shoulders puffing on a cigarette. He had little blue marks around his nose and on his cheeks, and as Holdorff passed him going into the liquor store, he could hear the subdued wheezing of his breathing. As he stood at the counter with a six-pack of Lucky Lager, he heard a song he'd

238

The Muttering Retreats

never heard before playing on the radio behind the counter. He stayed in the liquor store after he paid his ninety-nine cents for the beer so he could hear the song through. He had to listen to one more song before the deejay came on and told him the title of the first song he'd heard, "American Pie," by Don McLean.

"Wow!" he muttered to himself as he walked out of Bonesio's. "What a great song!"

As he walked back out to his car, the old man was standing on the corner waiting for the signal to change. He put the six-pack on the seat and climbed in next to it.

It was twilight as he drove along West Cliff Drive and all he could think of was the song he'd just heard. He didn't even notice that there were no surfers in the water at Steamer Lane. As he rounded the point, he got his last glimpse of blue turning purple on the sunless horizon, and by the time he reached his place, the sky was black. The other thing he couldn't get out of his mind was the afternoon's tryst, but by now he wasn't so preoccupied with it that he couldn't write.

Eight months till winter, and the thought of it made him long for the warm Southern California climate. He'd been thinking a lot lately about moving back there. In addition to the good weather, he was sure it would be easier to get gainful employment there because of his connections. Maybe get another job in the Long Beach schools. Be a chalk pusher again. Get back together with H.H. He'd be fifteen on his next birthday. Try to get him interested in something besides baseball. Something more intellectual. Literature, philosophy, politics. Mathematics even. The more he thought about it, the better he liked the idea.

He took the six-pack off the front seat and walked down the driveway to his garage apartment. The air inside his place was still heavy with the afternoon's lovemaking. One of the rare times when he could actually say his house was woman-smelling. The bed was still tousled, and he got an erection just thinking about the afternoon's activities there. He couldn't get over it. She really knew what she was doing when it came to sex. She'd even shown *him* a thing or two.

He walked the six-pack over to the refrigerator and put it in next to his bundles of manuscripts. He took one can out and went over to the typewriter. He hung his jacket over the back of the chair, sat down and began to shuffle through some of the canceled envelopes next to the typewriter. Then, still thinking about

240

The Muttering Retreats

"American Pie," he began to write. An hour later he had three cancelled envelopes filled with words. He pulled the typewriter in front of him and started transcribing the words:

Rebirth

I been rockin' 'n' rollin' since 'fifty-four,
Yeah, been doin' it till there ain't no more.
Now I'm a-waitin' for it to come back around,
Yeah, I'm a-lookin' for to be listenin' to that
    sound.
And it seemed that the music would never die,
Yeah, the melody's just got'a stick around.

From Fats to Buddy, the scene was thrivin'
We rocked around the clock, and we were
        hand jivin'.
Then the plane went down in fifty-nine,
Leaving the music to rot on the vine.
But the music just refuses to die;
It only ages like vintage wine.

Well, we twisted that long summer away,
And waited and watched as it all turned to clay.
We weren't sure we could wait it out,
But then in 'sixty-three, we began to twist and
    shout.
And the music just refuses to die,
Though sometimes it can't be figured out.

We got plenty of Satisfaction;

Smoke put us in the middle of the action.
When the air finally cleared, the scene was bi-
zarre;
Paul and Art rode off in the same car.
Yeah, the music just refuses to die,
Though nobody knows who they are.

I'm a-wonderin' what the seventies'll bring.
Will Dylan and the Dead still be doing their
thing?
I'll still be there as it lives on again,
Listenin' and singin' till the very end.
And the music just refuses to die
It'll be waitin' there around the bend.

And the music just refuses to die;
Yeah, the music just refuses to die.

(Repeat last)

When he finished, he sat and puffed on
his pipe and read his song/poem. He got up and
walked over to his radio on the nightstand next
to the bed and turned it on. Holdorff always had
it tuned to the same station, one that played a
good mix of rock 'n' roll. When the sound came
in, he was listening to the last verse of "Visions
of Johanna." He hadn't heard it in quite a while,
and the power of those metaphors still over-
whelmed him. The precision of the rhymes was
irresistible. Although, in a sense it depressed

242

The Muttering Retreats

him because it was hitting close to home. Holdorff the romantic. Letting his emotions get the best of him. Thinking about the woman he'd spent the afternoon with and hearing, "And Madonna, she still has not showed." He sang along with the seven consecutive rhymes after that line, and was awed at the mastery of it. And the words themselves, the story they told. Holdorff could relate to it. In a sense, he was seeing his own empty cage corrode. When he thought of what he must look like right at that moment, he shuddered, but he couldn't escape it, so he listened to and sang along while his own conscience exploded.

The telephone rang. It rang again. Holdorff looked at his clock and saw that it was nine-fifteen. Wondering who could be calling at that time on a Tuesday night, he walked over to the telephone and answered it in the middle of the third ring. Dylan's final harmonica solo mourned in the background as he spoke into the receiver. His ex-wife was on the other end, and her agitated voice bordered on hysteria. She was calling from Saint Mary's Hospital in Long Beach, the same hospital their son had been born in. She seemed reasonably calm at first, but as the story unfolded, she choked back the tears

243

and eventually just broke down and sobbed as Holdorff listened in stunned disbelief.

Their son had gone to a drive-in movie with his friend Johnny and his parents. H.H. had gone to the men's room by himself and didn't return, so Johnny's father went looking for him. He found him unconscious on the men's room floor with the middle finger on his right hand cut off at the knuckle. He'd apparently been beaten unconscious by a bigger kid a couple years older. Nobody knew for sure. There were no eyewitnesses. The other kid just disappeared into one of the cars, and he never came forward. H.H. had regained consciousness, and was in agonizing pain from his injury.

Holdorff told his ex-wife he'd leave immediately so that he could be with his son as early tomorrow morning as possible. After he hung up, he sat down and took a big pull from his beer. Then he put his face in his hands and did all he could to fight back the tears.

He sat at the kitchen table for about ten more minutes. Then he collected himself. He got out a paper bag with handles and began stuffing it with clothes from his dresser. Then he went over to the closet and pulled out his sleeping bag. When he got everything assembled in one place, he started some water boiling on the

The Muttering Retreats

stove. He took the two bags out to the car, opened the rear door and put them in. When he got back to the house, the water was boiling. He shut it off and put two heaping teaspoons of instant coffee into a cup. He poured the scalding water over the brown crystals and stirred them. He threw the spoon into the sink and picked up the cup and sipped. He started running hot water for the shower.

When he came out of the shower, he made himself another cup of coffee. He got the towel from the bathroom and stood near the wall heater to get his long hair and beard dry. One thing he didn't need right now was to catch a cold, so he made sure he was dry and comfortable for the drive south. He put on a gray short sleeve sweatshirt under his corduroy jacket. After he got his glasses on, he lit his pipe. When he finished the coffee, he poured himself one more for the road.

He made a quick scan of the room and saw the half empty can of beer on the table next to the typewriter. He took it to the sink and poured it out and threw the can away. He made sure that the refrigerator was shut tight. Cup of coffee in hand, pipe jutting out the corner of his mouth, he made his way out the front door, smoke trailing along behind him.

Jerome Arthur

Before going to the car, he stopped at the house out in front and left a note telling his landlord he'd be gone for a few days. He didn't know for sure when he'd be back, but he would be back.

This was his first trip to Southern California since he'd moved north. It had been almost two years since he'd last seen his son.

Nineteen

Holdorff drove through the night, pulled into Long Beach at six o'clock in the morning and went straight to Saint Mary's. He waited in a room with two expectant fathers for half an hour before they let him in to see H.H. It was the same room he'd waited in fourteen years before when H.H. was born. When he finally did get in to see him, the boy seemed to be in good spirits considering what he'd been through. He'd suffered a slight concussion, and was unconscious for about a half hour, which turned out to be nothing serious in light of the severed finger. The fact that he was unconscious when the punk cut it off probably made that injury less painful when it was happening. It acted as anesthesia. Johnny's dad did some quick thinking and got the finger into the refrigerator in the snack bar. When the ambulance arrived, the paramedics kept it cold as they transported H.H. and the finger to the hospital. It was successfully re-attached, but he only had limited mobility with it.

The one remaining question was what emotional effect all of this would have on H.H. It seemed to Holdorff that he was handling this part of it all right. His hopes of ever being a pitcher were dashed. He might be able to play another position that didn't require a lot of throwing, like right field or first base. He probably wouldn't play much baseball after he got out of high school anyway.

Holdorff was in Long Beach for the rest of the week, and he saw H.H. every day he was there. He spent his first three nights in town at Blake's place. She was still single living in her little bungalow on Nieto Avenue. He stayed with Tavisón Friday and Saturday and went home on Sunday.

On Friday morning before he went to visit H.H., who'd gone home from the hospital by then, he drove out to City and looked up Tavisón in his office. He made arrangements to stay with him those last two nights, and then he went over to H.H.'s house and spent the rest of that day and most of the next hanging with him.

He showed up back at Tavisón's office on Friday afternoon. He was glad to see that Tavisón hadn't changed a bit. Still the same af-

The Muttering Retreats

fable, down-to-earth guy whom he'd known sixteen years ago at the beginning of his academic odyssey, the same guy who'd told him to get into history, stay away from English, but who now didn't even remember giving that advice.

The last time they'd talked was that day they'd had a couple beers at the Forty Niners. Since then Tavisón had quit his job at City, moved to México, worked as a consultant with the National University for a year, and moved back to Long Beach.

"When I found out about the job in México, I asked for a year of unpaid leave, and they wouldn't give it to me, so I just quit."

"How long you been workin' here, anyway?"

"When I put in for the leave? Fourteen years."

"So, what happened in México? Why'd you come back?"

"My wife couldn't stand the heat down there. She moved back right away, and I followed when the job ended."

"You have any trouble getting back on at City?"

"Wasn't easy. Put my tail between my legs and begged for my job back."

"Wow, what a drag."

Jerome Arthur

This all happened within the last three years. Tavisón moved to México at the same time Holdorff was on his way to Santa Cruz.

"So, what've you been up to since the last time I saw you?"

"Got bounced outa' grad. school at S.C. and moved to Santa Cruz. Neat little beach town with a U.C. campus. Don't know how much longer I can go on, though. Been hanging around campus a couple years. Beautiful spot, and they're doing some interesting stuff academically, but it's tough to get in. Probably 'cause of the size of the place, and 'cause they got an easy grading system—written evaluations. *And* they got a great faculty, guys like Norman O. Brown. Undergraduates can go right up to him and talk to him. Don't think I can hang out much longer. Haven't had any kind of steady work since I've been there. Only income's my Navy pension. If I could get in, I'd get a T.A.-ship."

"The hell're written evaluations?"

"'Steada' giving letter grades, the teachers write up evaluations of students' work. 'Bout a paragraph long. Sometimes if you do really well, you'll get a longer evaluation."

"Sounds like a lota' paperwork to me. What's a transcript look like?"

The Muttering Retreats

"That's one a' the problems. Students seem to like it, though. Lota' people wan'a go there. And it's a nice little town, too. Hey, I only live a block from the beach, and it's never crowded like around here."

"So, what're your plans if you don't get into the doctoral program? You have to quit going to school sometime."

"Hey, if I haven't gotten in at Santa Cruz by now, I'm probably not go'n'a get in. I was over at the district office yesterday and picked up some application forms. Maybe start out subbing. Work into full-time. Hell, maybe move back no matter what. There's this situation with my boy. If he needs me, I'll move back just to be with him. He needs more male influence in his life. 'Least more'n his mother and grandma can give 'im."

"For what it's worth, I'd write you a recommendation, but it'd probably do you more harm than good."

"It'd be nice to get accepted at Santa Cruz, but you know, going to school *is* getting old. It really hit home last quarter when I was sitting in on an American novel class. Teacher was lecturing on *The Portrait of a Lady.* You know that one?"

"Oh, yeah."

251

Jerome Arthur

"Teacher lectured on the chapter where Osmond is proposing to Isabel. He describes the garish surroundings of the hotel sitting room where the proposal takes place—the yellow, orange, purple and gilt furnishings, the ostentation of the art work, the rosy nimbus of the setting, and how it all somehow parallels Osmond's character. And you know, I heard that lecture in the American lit. class I took at State eleven years ago. It was like déjà vu. I knew I'd been down that road before. How long can you examine this stuff with such intensity without covering ground you've already covered before? I was feeling senile, and that really scared me. Damn, I'm only thirty-eight, too young to be senile."

"You think you've got it bad. Think of how many times the teacher's not only heard it, but had to say it, too. If you're going to be in this trade, you've really got to think of ways to improvise to keep it interesting for yourself. It seems like the only kind of variety left is when you get a different batch of students each semester."

"Got'a be better'n what *I'm* doing. I'm going nowhere. Feel like I haven't made any headway since I got my B.A."

252

The Muttering Retreats

It was the first time Holdorff admitted it out loud, but he knew the feelings he'd just expressed were inside him all along.

"Teaching's got its good points," Tavisón interjected here. "Best part is the students, and of course, you get all the holidays and summers off. Pay's getting better. I don't think it'll ever be competitive with comparable jobs on the outside, but then that's a whole other argument."

"Maybe it's what I need to make my life more stable. I'm startin' to feel middle age comin' on. It'll be my last stand, and I'd better make it good, 'cause so far I haven't made good on anything I've tried."

"You underestimate your accomplishments. You've come a long way from the first remedial English class you took from me. How long ago was that?"

Holdorff thought for a minute. "Eighteen years ago, almost nineteen. Fall semester 'fifty-two. Still in the Navy. Hardly seems possible. That's what I'm talking about. Seventeen years of school and all I've got to show for it is a B.A. degree and three bundles of poems and song lyrics in my ice box. Same place financially. If anything, I'm in worse shape financially. In those days I had my G.I. benefits *and* my pen-

253

sion. Now all I've got's my pension. Don't have any steady, consistent relationship with a woman. My home isn't much better'n my car. Only family's my son, and he's probably go'n'a be screwed up for the rest of his life 'cause of some fuckin' punk at the drive-in movie. That boy and the poems in the ice box are about my only accomplishments."

"You berate yourself too much. You're an honest-to-god intellectual. There are people on the inside who don't know as much about T.S. Eliot as you do. More who haven't written nearly as much as you."

"That may be true, but what do I really know? Hell, people tell me everyday that I'm missing good stuff on T.V., but as far as I'm concerned, there isn't anything on T.V. that's worth watching, but judging from what most people are saying, you'd think that everything that happens, happens on television. Political conventions, Olympic games, summer and winter, situation comedy, game shows, soap operas. I think it's all bullshit, but a nation is tuned to it, and loving every minute of it. What do I know? T.S. Eliot, Allen Ginsberg.

"I remember when I used to work in the clinic up at State how I used to tell the other T.A.s it was all bullshit, but I don't think I really

The Muttering Retreats

believed it then. I was just kidding mostly, but now I actually think it's true. Even my own writing seems like bullshit. On rainy days, I sit at my typewriter, the hollow sound of the rain beating on my roof, the hollow sound of the keys hitting the paper in the carriage, and I wonder what it's all for.

"I feel like the guy I saw playing guitar and singing on the street in Santa Cruz. I was in a bar looking out the window at him. He was sitting on a stool with the guitar resting on his crossed legs, and I could see his fingers picking at the strings and his lips moving behind his full beard and mustache, but I couldn't hear a thing from where I sat in the bar. He had no audience on the street. In fact, I think I was the only person paying any attention to him, and I couldn't even hear him. Like watching a silent movie without captions. I was by myself and sipping my beer, watching this silent mannequin with animated lips and fingers. The futility of it gave me a cold shiver. I wished somebody would stop and at least listen or maybe even keep time with the music, but no one did. If anything, the passers-by seemed to quicken their pace as they passed him. The longer I watched, the more depressed I got, so that when I finished my beer, I didn't have the stomach to order another one. I had to get out of there, and when I did, I found *myself* quickening my own pace as I walked by him. His strains faded once again into silence as I turned the corner and headed home to play *my* music on my typewriter to an empty house. And where did my song go? Into the silent confines of the refrigerator."

"You know how many people would like to write just one poem? You've got a whole re-frigerator full of them. You know how many times I've tried to write something, anything, and not finished it? And I'm supposed to be a skilled master of the English language. That'll tell you something about what it's like on the inside. Scholars and teachers would give their eyeteeth for your literary achievement.

"Listen. You know how teachers fulfill their need to be creative? Let me tell you what I do. I play popular songs on a phonograph while the class reads the lyrics on dittos that I type up myself. There's a full-time secretary for the de-partment who's supposed to type them up, but she works for ten other teachers besides me. I don't mind typing them up. In fact, I think it's the closest I'll ever come to doing any writing myself. By typing out the words, I feel almost like I'm writing the songs. Even that process gets boring. I end up searching for material else-

elsewhere. I've already used Shakespeare's 'Sonnet Eighteen,' 'The Jaberwokie,' and 'The Death of a Ball Turret Gunner' until I not only know the poems by heart, but also know what I'm going to say about them to the last word. Now the process is repeating itself with 'The Dangling Conversation' and 'Gentle on my Mind.' You know those two songs?"

"Yeah, Paul Simon wrote the first one and John Hartford wrote the second. I'm a song writer myself, remember?"

"I know you're sending stuff out all the time. You've got to keep on doing it. Something's going to break for you. It's got to."

"But I haven't sold a scrap. Writing it is one thing. Getting it published is another thing altogether."

"You're an artist. You shouldn't have to concern yourself with the commercial part of it. Look, all I'm saying is that you've done quite a lot since you started out eighteen years ago, and you should feel a sense of achievement no matter how little it's appreciated by anybody else. 'So long as men can breathe or eyes can see,/So long lives this, and this gives life to thee.'"

As Tavisón gathered the things he wanted to take home for the weekend, his office door swung open, and Steinberg popped her head in.

"Did I miss a faculty meeting today?" she asked.

"You're far too obsessive to miss anything," Tavisón replied in a jocular tone.

He winced as he looked over at Holdorff who was already wincing as he recognized Steinberg's hatchet sharp features.

"Seriously," Steinberg said.

"No, you didn't miss a faculty meeting."

She didn't seem to recognize Holdorff at first, and he didn't encourage her. He didn't want to say anything to her unless he had to. He turned slightly sideways, not wanting to be recognized, but the move only called him to Steinberg's attention. She looked more closely at him through her tinted horn rim glasses, and reacting as though she had a sudden burst of insight, she said,

"Holdoff! I haven't seen you in years."

"It's Holdorff, Steinberg," he said coolly, "and it hasn't been long enough for my money."

"Whatever. How've you been? What're you doing these days?"

"I'm A.B.D. at U.C. Santa Cruz," he lied.

The Muttering Retreats

He couldn't bring himself to tell her the truth. It would have been too humiliating, and he knew she would shriek it up and down the halls. He glanced at Tavisón out of the corner of his eye and was gratified to see that his lie brought no reaction from him.

"I heard what happened to you up at S.C. Too bad."

Her tone was more one of dismissal than of sympathy. It was obvious to Holdorff that she didn't give a damn what his situation was. She was just making conversation, and not idle conversation, but disparaging talk designed to put him down. Lording it over him. That was always her specialty before, and it hadn't appeared to change now.

"I'm A.B.D. at Chapman. In fact, I've only got to write a conclusion and my dissertation will be done. It's on the poetic diction of Coleridge as demonstrated in *Biographia Literaria*. Dense stuff. What's yours on?"

"Oh, I really haven't started the actual writing yet, but I'm go'n'a do something with T.S. Eliot." Then turning to Tavisón, he said, "Didn't you say your wife was go'n'a have dinner early? Shouldn't we be hittin' the road pretty soon?"

Jerome Arthur

He was looking for any excuse he could think of to get out from under the magnifying glass of Steinberg's derogatory chatter.

"Yeah. We really do have to run."

As they walked out to the parking lot where Tavisón's 'fifty-three Chevy was parked, Holdorff was struck by the changes on campus since the last time he'd been there. There were a few new buildings, a new cafeteria among them.

Holdorff said, "A lota' changes on campus, but Steinberg hasn't changed a bit. Still a shrill know-it-all."

"You ought to hear her at the faculty meetings. Everybody thinks she's a pain in the ass. Guys I feel sorry for are the ones who share an office with her. She'd drive me nuts if she were in my office."

"Sounds about like how it was in the clinic. She'd come around and everybody'd head the other way. Even the kind, considerate ones. I remember this one miss-goodie-two-shoes. Don't remember her name now, but she used to be so sweet and innocent she wouldn't say 'shit' if she had a mouthful. One time when she saw Steinberg coming our way, she got this sour look on her face and walked away. She sure has a way of bringing out the worst in people. A real breath of stale air."

The Muttering Retreats

"She sure has got the brass around here snowed. And who knows? She might be a good teacher. I've never seen her perform, and I haven't heard much about her from the students."

"Oh, I'm sure she knows her stuff. She did in the clinic, but she had a lousy rapport with the students and other clinicians. My car's right over here on the street."

"Ever been to my place?"

"No. I'll follow you when you come outa' the parking lot."

"Okay."

As Holdorff pulled away from the campus, he looked over at the bus stop bench where he'd offered his ex-wife a ride on that fateful day so many years ago. He could almost remember the time when he was so young and eager. He never thought then that he'd end up where he was now, just as he couldn't possibly guess now where he'd be fifteen years hence. Suddenly he became painfully aware of the contrast between himself and Tavisón. Whereas he couldn't possibly have guessed that he'd be where he was now or where he'd be in the future, almost by nature Tavisón could be assured of where he was at every moment in the present and where he'd be at any given point in the future.

Jerome Arthur
Twenty minutes later they pulled up in front of Tavisón's house in Rossmoor.

Twenty

Holdorff and Tavisón had an early dinner and then spent the rest of the evening talking in Tavisón's home office. By ten o'clock they were both yawning heavily.

"About time to hit the sack," said Tavisón as they stepped out into the hall and went upstairs. He pointed to the room across the hall. "Make yourself comfortable in here. Bathroom's the next-door down. See you in the morning. Now let's see. You're going to want to go see H.H. in the morning, right?"

"Yeah."

When you get back here, we can go down to the Shore wander around, see what's happening. How long's it been since you've been there?"

"I spent the last couple nights there with my lady friend, Blake. Before that? Long time. Last time I actually hung out down there was back when I was going to S.C. I see where they changed the name of the A & P to Shopping Bag."

"Don't know. Haven't been down that way lately myself. Well, I'll see you in the morning. Got'a get some shuteye. I'm beat."

Holdorff could hear Tavisón's footsteps padding down the carpeted hall toward his bedroom. He went into the bathroom and brushed his teeth. Tavisón's wife was such a good housekeeper that Holdorff felt uneasy using the clean toilet. He had half a notion to sneak out into the back yard and piss in the flowerbed, but he didn't. He used the toilet and went back to his room and fell asleep as soon as his head hit the pillow.

Holdorff didn't wake up till almost eight o'clock the next morning. Tavisón's wife fixed them some breakfast and Holdorff was out the door by ten. H.H.'s hand was hurting pretty badly and the boy was weak and exhausted from the pain, so he only hung out with him till about one o'clock, and H.H. slept most of that time. When he left the hospital, he drove back over to Tavisón's place. They got down to the Shore around two-thirty and stopped in the Alcapulco and the Beachcomber and had a couple beers. After that they drove down to Ocean Boulevard at Belmont Pier and went along the beach to

The Muttering Retreats

Bay Shore. From there Tavisón took them to the Forty Niners.

By the time they got to the bar, it was three-thirty and the place wasn't busy at all. In fact, they were the only people in the joint. As they passed through the front door, Holdorff felt like he was walking into a time capsule. The only thing that was different in the bar since the last time he'd been there was the bartender. All the old western artifacts were still there, from the spurs and bits decorating the wall behind the bar to the old, spider web-festooned wagon wheel that hung from the ceiling in the middle of the room. The coin-operated pool table to the left of the bar seemed, as it always had, somehow out of place.

They sat down at the bar and ordered a couple beers. Then they moved over to the pool table and started a game. The bartender put fifty cents into the jukebox and "Aquarius" from *Hair* blasted out. Holdorff sang along with it. He liked the tune, but he didn't care for what he thought was the hippy philosophy implicit in it. While he sang, Tavisón kept his distance, always managing to be at the opposite end of the pool table. When they finished their beers, Holdorff suggested they get a pitcher. Tavisón won the first game and they started another.

Jerome Arthur

"I've been married too long," Tavisón said. "You're lucky you don't have to answer to anybody. Come and go as you please. Do things on the slightest whim."

"And when it's all over, go home to an empty house, an empty bed," Holdorff said with a grim expression on his face.

Then suddenly the woman he'd had sex with on Tuesday came to mind.

"I guess the only thing to be said for being married is that the sex is steady, but hard to get and boring once gotten."

"But steady nonetheless," replied Holdorff.

Midway through the third game, someone walked in the door and went up to the bar. Holdorff was shooting at the time, so he didn't see that it was McSwayne until after he looked up from the game. McSwayne's eyes hadn't adjusted to the darkness, so he didn't recognize Holdorff at first. Even after he could see better, he didn't recognize him because in the six years since he'd last seen him, Holdorff's hair had gotten longer and was starting to go gray. He looked different. Holdorff recognized McSwayne as soon as he turned to look at the pool game.

The Muttering Retreats

"Well, I'll be damned!" said Holdorff. "Hey McSwayne. What're you doin' still hanging around here? Thought you'd be in Grass Valley by now."

"I *am* in Grass Valley."

"All right! You get a job?"

"Got a couple classes at American River J.C. outside Sacramento. Only work Tuesday and Thursday."

"You ever get tenure at State?"

"Nope. I got passed over again, so I just quit and moved north."

"How 'bout your wife?"

"Stayed here."

"You guys split up?"

"No. Someone in the family's got'a work. She's finishing out her last year at City. Go'n'a have a full load at American River in the fall. We're moving her up in June. Been doing alternate weekends back and forth. I drive down to see her, and she flies up to see me. I came down yesterday. Headin' back Monday morning. We did get a place in Maui. Spend Christmas and Easter there. She comes to Grass Valley summers. How the hell you been? What're you doin' these days?"

"Living up north, too. Know where Santa Cruz is?"

"Near Monterey?"

"That's it. Just north. I'm tryin' to get into the Ph.D. program at the U.C. campus there. Wha'da yuh got at the J.C. where you work?"

"Two classes I told yuh about. Got my real estate license, so I'm doin' a little bit a' that part-time. Spare time, I'm growin' a vegetable garden."

Holdorff introduced McSwayne to Tavisón. Tavisón knew McSwayne's wife, but not well. They spent the next couple hours talking over old times and drinking pitchers of beer. Holdorff and McSwayne congratulated each other on how lucky they were to be living in their respective parts of Northern California. Tavisón had no comment.

At length all three of them went out to hit some bars down in the Shore. By this time they were already half lit, so the bright sunlight hit them like a freight train when they stepped outside. McSwayne left his car parked and climbed into the back seat of Tavisón's. Once in the Shore, they didn't prolong their stay in any one bar, but rather had one beer in four different joints. By seven o'clock they were all three snockered and ready to go home. Tavisón dropped McSwayne off at the Forty Niners, and

The Muttering Retreats

as he and Holdorff drove off, they saw him go back into the bar rather than to his car. Tavisón drove slowly and carefully off down Seventh Street past State and out to Rossmoor.

When they got back to his house, his wife raged around the kitchen preparing something to eat. In his intoxicated state, Tavisón tried to be affectionate, but she was having none of it. Holdorff would have felt uneasy, but he was too drunk to care, so he sat in the corner and, getting comfortable, began to nod off. Before he could doze off completely, Tavisón's wife served up some chili, which he and Tavisón attacked voraciously, it being the only thing they'd eaten since the Specials they'd had at the Forty Niners. When they'd gotten their fill, they went out onto the patio in back and sat down in a couple of chaise lounges. Within minutes they were both sound asleep.

When Holdorff woke up, it was dark and he was alone on the patio. It was warm, the sky was dark, and stars twinkled above. When he got to his feet, Tavisón's wife confronted him.

"What time are you planning on leaving tomorrow?" She couldn't have been more terse or to the point. "I'll have breakfast ready by eight. You can join us and have coffee afterward, but I'm afraid I have plans for my husband for the rest of the day, so I'd appreciate it if you could be on your way before noon."

It was the most she'd said to him since he met her.

"How's he feeling?" Holdorff asked.

"Not bad, considering how much both of you must've drunk. He's in bed."

"Think I'll go for a walk."

"I'll leave the kitchen door unlocked so you can get in when you get back."

He went out into the dark night. The streets of the neighborhood were deserted, and as he walked along dragging on his pipe, he saw the blue light of the television sets humming behind the curtained windows of almost every house, and once again he felt all alone. Looking up into the sky, he was reminded of his puniness and he remembered when he was a kid how he used to look at the night sky in fear and wonder, trying to understand it, childlike, innocent. He didn't understand it then and he didn't understand it now, but he knew he was seeing the same thing that astronomers saw and understood twenty-five hundred years ago. Mars and Venus, the Big Dipper, the North Star, and Orion. Then he remembered how he'd heard that some stars are so far away that by the time we see them here on earth, they're already burned out. Thus,

The Muttering Retreats

at the very moment he was looking at a star, it no longer existed, and so also were stars disappearing from the heavens as Anaximander gazed at them.

As he walked, he watched the lights go out one by one in the houses he passed. By the time he got back to Tavisón's place, very few lights were still on in the neighborhood. As he entered through the kitchen door, all the lights were out except a lone night light on the stove. He turned the overhead light on, hung his jacket on a chair, got a canceled envelope out of his breast pocket, sat down at the kitchen table, and began to write:

Seems I've Run Dry

It seems that I've run dry
So I ask myself why
Do I persist in this—
Surely not for bliss.

(Refrain)
Call me what you will:
Slow learner, late to fulfill
My skill, standing still
Till I lose the thrill.

Wait patiently for the flow,
And though it comes so slow,

Jerome Arthur

I know it'll come back,
And I'll write like a maniac.
(Refrain)

Now the talking'll cease;
Go'n'a pack it in a valise.
Words've all gone away,
To return another day.
(Refrain)

Twenty-one

Holdorff was up by seven the next morning, and he heard the commotion of Sunday morning breakfast outside his half closed door. He couldn't hear anybody talking, but he could smell the bacon cooking downstairs. The shower was going in the master bathroom down the hall. He got out of bed and rubbed the cobwebs from his eyes. He was feeling the effects of yesterday's carousing with Tavisón. He pulled his trousers on and went into the bathroom and splashed some water on his face. Then he lit his pipe and took three big drags before setting it next to the ashtray on the nightstand next to his bed. He buttoned his shirt and tucked it in. He and Tavisón stepped into the hallway at the same time. When they got to the kitchen, Tavisón's wife was at the stove.

"'Mornin' honey," Tavisón said as he kissed her on the cheek.

"'Morning."

He poured two cups of coffee, gave one to Holdorff and led him out onto the patio. They sat down, sipped their coffee and talked.

"What time you figure to get home to-day?" Tavisón asked.

"Don't know for sure. Depends on what time I get outa' here. Go'n'a stop by and check in one last time with H.H. See if he's feeling any better today. I won't be pushing it on the road. Probably make a lota' stops. I got a pretty good hangover."

The truth was that he'd probably push it because he wanted to get home, get showered, and get into his own bed. He'd had a good stay in Long Beach, and he really didn't feel like he'd been away from home. After seeing H.H., Blake, Tavisón and McSwayne, it was more like going back home. In fact, it might *be* home again. It depended to a large extent on what U.C.S.C. did. He knew he wouldn't stay in Santa Cruz if he didn't get accepted at the school.

It *was* a nifty little town with good weather and nice beaches, but there were times when Holdorff didn't think that compensated for the cold winters. And if his son really needed him in Long Beach, he knew he'd have to move back. He didn't want to think about these things now. All he was thinking at that moment was getting something into his stomach and getting back on the road.

"If it'll make you feel any better," Tavisón told Holdorff as he led him around to the side of the house where there was a huge pile of twisted ivy and dried out eugenias, "here's what I'm doin' today. It's been piled up here for quite a while. Wife won't get off my back till I get busy on it."

Tavisón's wife called out to them that breakfast was ready, so they went into the kitchen and sat down at the table. Nobody talked much, and when he finished his second cup of coffee, Holdorff went back to the bedroom and gathered his things.

By nine-thirty he was back in his Sedan Delivery and on his way north. He wanted to take one last quick swing through the Shore on his way over to see H.H. As he drove along Second Street, he saw Novak coming out of Howie's Market. He had a small paper bag tucked under his arm. Novak turned the corner and Holdorff turned with him. He pulled up alongside as Novak was getting into his car. The window on that side was already down, so Holdorff called out:

275

"Hey, Novak. The hell's goin' on?"

Novak looked a little confused as he turned around, but when he recognized Holdorff, he smiled and leaned in the window to shake hands.

"I don't believe it," he said. "How many years 's it been? Where the hell you been hiding?"

"I only made two moves since the last time I saw you. Up to S.C. for four years. Came away empty-handed. No Ph.D. Now I'm in Santa Cruz. Know where that is?"

"Yeah. What're you doing up there?"

"Tryin' to get into grad. school. Got a U.C. campus there. Been in town since Tuesday. Remember H.H., my son?"

"Yeah."

"He was attacked by some punks last Tuesday at the drive-in."

"No kiddin'! Hurt bad?"

"Lost a finger. Middle finger, right hand. Well, he didn't really lose it. The adult he was with knew enough to get it on ice, so they re-attached it. It's not a hundred percent, but it'll work. I was just on my way over to see him right now when I saw you. Headin' back to Santa Cruz after that. What're you up to?"

The Muttering Retreats

"I'm still teaching up on the hill. Say listen, I can't stop and talk right now. I've got this lady waiting for me, and if I'm to expect her to spend the day with me, I'd better get back and fix her some breakfast. Why don't we get together later on?"

"Can't. I was just heading out of town. Gi'me that bag a sec.," Holdorff said, taking out a pen. He wrote his name, address and phone number down on the bag Novak was carrying. "If you're ever up my way, gi'me a call. I got a nice pad. I can put you up."

He could hear himself saying it, but he knew he'd never see Novak in Santa Cruz, and even if he did, he knew he wouldn't stay with *him*. Novak was too clean cut for Holdorff's style of living.

"I might do that," said Novak taking the bag back and looking at what Holdorff had written on it. "Well, take it easy, Holdorff. I hope you get into that program you're trying for."

"Yeah. I do too. Really, if you do get up my way, give me a call. See you later." And he rumbled off down the street

*   *   *

Jerome Arthur

Holdorff was back in Santa Cruz for about a week when he got the letter from Long Beach City Schools inviting him to the district office to be interviewed for a job teaching freshman English at Poly High for spring semester. He'd come back around to where he'd started. He saw the offer as an opportunity to be rescued from his present circumstances. The student life bored him anymore. It had lost its charm. Ultimately, all he really wanted to do was write poems. He did want to make some money in the process, and the money on this job wasn't great, but it was enough. He knew that of all the things he'd done, teaching had the most to offer him (the interaction with the students and the time off, for example), but he also knew that it had the potential for being the most boring.

He decided right then and there that he'd go ahead and move back to Long Beach when he went down for his interview. That night he went to the house in front and gave his landlord notice. The next morning he called the district and set up an appointment for an interview in three weeks. He spent the rest of the time getting his things together. He'd rented his place furnished, so he didn't have to move any furniture. The only thing of his that could be called

278

The Muttering Retreats

furniture was the Webcor. That and the Underwood were the heaviest, bulkiest things he had. His car had just about enough room for those and all of his other personal belongings. On the Monday before the interview, he packed everything in the car and started on his way south on Highway One.

The End   1979-2016

About the Author

Jerome Arthur grew up in Los Angeles, California. He lived on the beach in Belmont Shore, a neighborhood in Long Beach, California, for nine years in the 1960s. He and his wife Janet moved to Santa Cruz, California in 1969. These three cities are the settings for his ten novels.